Lincolnshire
COUNTY COUNCIL

discover libraries

**This book should be returned on or before
the due date.**

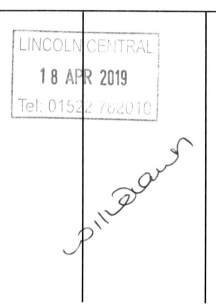

LINCOLN CENTRAL

1 8 APR 2019

Tel: 01522 782010

es

To renew or order library books please telephone 01522 782010
or visit https://lincolnshire.spydus.co.uk

You will require a Personal Identification Number.
Ask any member of staff for this.

The above does not apply to Reader's Group Collection Stock.

Published in 2011 by New Generation Publishing

First Edition

www.newgenerationpublishing.info

Acknowledgment

I would like to sincerely thank my editor Jenny Rowley for her help and kindness. Despite her busy life she kindly volunteered to do the editing which I am grateful for. Also I would like to thank Ros Franey for her further assistance and guidance.

Introduction

When I finished the first draft of this story I knew I had ended up with a complex narrative. As we all know, dreams and nightmares don't follow a straight and logical sequence. In nightmares, time and space are mixed and events don't happen in an orderly fashion. An event can happen anytime, anywhere and can have a surreal nature. This is a recipe for complexity. This story is also told through the mind of a person who has suffered a mental illness, which again adds to its convoluted nature. I have tried to accurately portray political, social, cultural and environmental situations and at the same time reveal a little of my own life story. The narrative is multi-layered; it describes situations in many different environments. In order to reduce its complexity, I decided to break it into six parts or chapters.

Part (1): "Nightmarish Realities" In this part I describe nothing but reality. Everything in this part happened in reality. In this part I include aspects of my own biography to give the reader more knowledge and understanding of my personal experience. This section is structured in the style of a journalist's report to emphasise the actual facts and events in the particular environments.

Part (2): "Real Nightmares" starts with nightmares which seem strange and surreal. This is an indication of the 'madness' which is a direct result of the brutal environment described in part 1.

Part (3): "Hopeless Human with Terrifying Nightmares" I tried to illustrate one reality; the fact that a hopeless human under severe pressure and living in intense fear tends to rely on escapism; seeking refuge in a safe haven / fantasies / religion for example, in order to continue living and surviving.

Part (4): "Human with Endless Nightmares Seeks Cure" This part is really about entering a new environment that is far removed from the previous brutal environment that a person used to live in. In my personal life this was the time when I escaped to western society as a refugee and got a chance to get help, thanks to the NHS: free of charge, funded by tax payers.

Part (5): "Nightmares are turning to dreams / fantasies and creativities" In this part I tried to illustrate that with care and a more humane environment, even an individual who has suffered terrifying experiences and mental illness can put his/her feet on a creative path. I also believe (in line with many psychologists) that the borders of madness and creativity are not far from each other. In this story I tried to describe a form of mental illness that I had suffered. Two main symptoms of that illness are: intense fear of persecution (the reader can witness this throughout the story) and wild association of thought. Ability to connect the thoughts, events, ideas…etc is also characteristic of a creative work of art. So if a sufferer manages to turn these wild associations of thought into a creative process, it can produce powerful - and sometimes harrowing - works of art. This part exists independently as a story in its own right but is actually an amalgamation of characters and events from several novels that I had already written. This is a complete and independent story and readers don't need to know about my previous novels. I just wanted to illustrate that proper use of the association of thoughts (or in this case my previous novels) can be a channel to creative work.

In fact, creative individuals have often sought to cultivate something very close to the schizophrenic experience as a way into their work. The French modernist poet Arthur Rimbaud proclaimed that poetry must proceed by a "systematic derangement of all the senses". And M.E. McGrath said: "Should I let anyone know that there are moments in schizophrenia that are 'special'? Where there's a different sort of vision allowed me? It's as if… I've gone around the corner of humanity to witness another world where my seeing, hearing and touching are intensified, and every thing is a wonder… I won't tell myself it's all craziness."

Part (6): "Back to Nightmarish Realities, Wiser" is about coming out of nightmares and again facing a difficult situation, but this time stronger and wiser.

I hope this introduction makes the story easier to follow and more enjoyable to read.

Mark Hill (M.Ofogh)

Part (1)
Nightmarish Realities
(Happened in real life)

Location: Kurdistan. It is a region that lies between several countries (Iran, Iraq, Turkey, Russia and Syria). For a long time, the Kurdish people have been struggling for freedom, independence and the right to be self-governing.

I remember the first time I went to Kurdistan. I was with my best friend, Seerous. Both of us were escapee army officers and we had to conduct a secret life to avoid being captured by the Iranian authorities. My friendship with Seerous began at Army University where we were both students. He was very honest and full of passion for freedom. Although our concepts of freedom and democracy were limited and mixed with the romance of revolution, there was something that we all knew and felt within our skin and bones: the brutality of the Islamic regime. I had great respect for his honesty and his bravery in standing up against the Islamic regime. He had managed to be in contact with an opposition group while we were at Army University, and several times we managed to write political messages on the walls and distribute some leaflets secretly. We could have ended up in prison, tortured and executed. I personally didn't know much about any of the opposition groups, but I admired them and, like many other young people, it was mainly passion and feeling that drove us and motivated us to join the opposition, rather than knowledge or logic. We both escaped from the army and for several months led a fugitive life. Living like fugitives was very difficult. We couldn't trust anyone, and we were always in fear of being arrested by the police or by secret agents. Every knock on our door, the ringing of a phone, any sound from our neighbours or even a person passing by terrified us. We were in constant fear and paranoid of getting arrested by the authorities. People in the west may think a fugitive is a person who has committed a crime and is on the run, and that the worst case scenario for a fugitive is to be captured and get a life sentence behind bars. In Iran any political activist – or even anybody that simply doesn't want to participate in the Dictator's policies - will inevitably become a fugitive soon or later, and if they are captured, they face torture and the prospect of a painful death. Once we tried to escape to Turkey. Seerous had found a smuggler who could give us false passports and take us to Turkey, but he took some money and disappeared. Eventually we managed to escape to Kurdistan; I couldn't believe that ordinary people would risk their own lives to help escapees and political activists. They welcomed us with open arms, and despite suffering from poverty, were generous and hospitable. War and the brutality of the regimes had not destroyed their bravery and kindness.

Time: During the war between Iran and Iraq (Summer of 1987to Summer of 1988). There was 8 years of war (1981-1988) between these two countries.

Region: In the mountains along the border between these two warring countries, a region where the weather is usually extreme, very cold in autumn and winter with lots of snow, rainy in spring and summer and with a constant wind that increased at certain times to storm and gales.

People: The only people we encountered in this particular region belonged to warring political groups. These groups were all opposed to Iran's regime and used this mountainous region as a base for their operations. Iranian agents were constantly coming there to find out the latest situation. Iraq's army was stationed not far away.

Borders have always been ideal places for smugglers, and in that area they were in constant movement. They smuggled many different things; carpets, gold, cigarettes, whisky, humans...etc

Spies were prevalent too, because they could gather information about their opponent's army and its capabilities, keep an eye on any opposing political groups and then, of course, sabotage and kill their members. There were three types of spy: those working for Iran, those working for Iraq and those working for both countries; double agents. Thus, when you encountered a person it was very difficult to know if that person was a spy, a smuggler, a member of one of the various political groups or just an ordinary person passing by.

The nearest village was at least a couple of hours walk from us, but there were small huts and shelters scattered around. Whole families lived in these temporary homes, most of them working for smugglers, providing them with food and a resting place. Close to our base was a coffee shop run by several brothers and their families who were involved in the smuggling business. Because they had good relations with all the political parties, these brothers were useful for differentiating spies from smugglers and also knew the region very well.

Health service: There was not a single doctor or nurse in the area. The only treatment we could get came from political groups whose members knew a little bit about drugs (supplied to them by the Iranian or Iraqi authorities) and could perform whatever injections were available. Our group of twenty in that base had a so-called 'medical staff' of two, and these two were visited by sick people from around the area, most of whom believed, bizarrely, that the injections that caused the greatest pain, particularly in their arms or buttocks, provided the best cure. While all of us were infested with lice, I was luckier than some because I was so sweaty and the salt from my sweat meant that I could keep the lice at bay for a bit longer, but everybody got them in the end; it was inevitable.

Main Events: for a period of several months we were under constant shelling from the Iranian army; in addition to this, poisoning the drinking water, planting mines and other acts of terrorism by Iranian spies, were common. We had only one shelter that could protect us from shells. Whenever shelling began everyone would run there, including our members, and the people from the coffee shop, but I usually remained outside because we needed to protect the shelter and prevent our enemies from tossing a grenade inside, which would kill everyone. It was terrifying not to take shelter with the other people, especially during those times when the army used what they called timed explosive shells, which could be exploded ten or fifteen metres above the ground, so that debris from them could fall anywhere.

For several months we lived in tents; each tent could be occupied by five or six people. We were in constant fear of a shell landing too close for us to have enough time to get to our shelter. Nights also were bad, because the fear of ground attack and shelling was just as great. Sometimes the army would put us under even more severe mental pressure by shooting one shell an hour all night, thereby depriving us of sleep and forcing us constantly back and forth between our tents and the shelter.

Biography: As far back as I can remember, whether writing or speaking, relating the details of my life has always been my response to interrogations. I've had to go through interrogation many times in my life. I've never had an interview that wasn't an interrogation. When I was in the army, I was questioned several times by the authorities. They wanted to find out if I was working with or had sympathy for any political group. These interrogations were carried out by many different people at different levels, from my immediate commander to different

8

organisations within the army. When I finally escaped from the army into Iraq, the interrogations continued, this time in Iraqi prisons and camps. I do not know why my past and present life was so important, although the excuses offered were always "Reasons of security", of course. Even after about 2 years, despite having told everything about myself already, I was asked again by members of our group to write about my past life. Why? I don't know. For what it's worth, here again I offer the highlights of my wonderful life.

I was born into a poor family in Tehran. I have two brothers and one sister. I think my father's biggest mistake was marrying my mother. He was forty when he got married to my mother who was only thirteen at the time. That sort of marriage is typical and is a widespread injustice not only for the women of Iran but also for most of the Muslim population all over the world. Fanatical ideas about women on the one hand and poverty and ignorance on the other make the situation extremely difficult for women. I grew up in a family in which there were constant arguments and fighting between my parents. On top of the poverty and my dysfunctional family, until I was ten I also suffered a physical disability. I had problems in both my legs and I wasn't able to walk properly which made me subject to bullying by the kids in my neighbourhood and at school. It was a bitter experience and I suffered tremendously. Children can be very cruel and I suffered from their bullying and harassment, both physically and verbally. At the age of thirteen, when the Shah was still in power, I joined a military high school; a boarding school with harsh discipline. Although, like many teenagers, I liked uniforms and guns, poverty was the main reason that drove me to go to military high school.

We were subjected to a very harsh regime and at the same time we had to study. The school authorities kept us away from ordinary people by confining us in a military base. They were preparing and educating us in a way that suited their regime only. Our soft and fragile characters must be reformed and shaped to fit their purpose. We were simply child soldiers. Discipline was very hard. For example, first year students weren't allowed to walk; they must run all the time. We were subjected to physical and mental punishment by officers and senior students. The military exercise, horrible food, lack of sleep and tiredness, detention and punishment, as well as the demands of carrying on studying at the same time were very tough.

I didn't know much about the Islamic movement then, but a couple of times sneaked out to join the protesters in the streets of Tehran. For me and the other students in the school, the Islamic revolution came to power with bullets, tear gas and blood. We were kept in school and didn't know that the Shah's regime was about to collapse. Even on the day of the Islamic revolution's victory, we didn't know what was going on, and the school's authorities tried hard to prevent us learning the truth. In order to keep us busy, they arranged a football match. On that afternoon, the invasion of school began, and officers and soldiers were ordered by the head of school to resist. We were ordered to stay in our classrooms while some of the officers and soldiers were fighting against the invaders. I remember some officers refused to defend the school and use their guns against the invaders. Only two top officers - the commander of the school and his deputy- and some of the soldiers were actually resisting and shooting. For several hours a massive attack was staged on us from every direction, until the invaders managed to occupy the school using guns, tear gas and Molotov cocktails. Five soldiers were killed inside the school and many civilians were killed outside. I can still remember clearly the death of one soldier who was killed on the roof of a building and his blood was pouring down through a drainpipe.

The commander of the school managed to escape disguised in a cook's uniform but his deputy was captured later on. The Revolutionary court ordered him to be executed. I remember there was another officer who also was arrested. Some students and soldiers falsely testified against him and accused him of resisting and shooting at the invaders. But we knew that it wasn't true; I personally saw him on the same day and he didn't participate in any shooting. With the help of his wife, I managed to find all the witnesses and talk to them and convinced them to stop lying. Most of them simply didn't like the officer and didn't really know that their false testimonies could lead to his execution. Some of them hadn't even been there on the day of the invasion. Revolutionary courts, with their rapid and unjustified orders, are responsible for killing lots of innocent people. For me and many others the Islamic revolution's victory began and continued with blood, death and dictatorship.

A year after military high school, I got a place in the army university, another disciplinarian boarding academy. While I was there the war between Iran and Iraq started. Immediately drafted into it, I served for five years on the front line, experiencing every kind of pain, devastation and madness. Briefly I include some of my experiences here. I say briefly because I can talk and write for ever about war and its profound effects on my life. Here are some of my experiences:

It was the beginning of the war between Iran and Iraq. We were young and inexperienced. The days in the desert were so hot – more than fifty degrees centigrade – and the only shady place was underneath the oil pipes. But the sound of the canons reverberated terribly in the pipes, and at night we had a bigger problem, the fucking mosquitoes. Sometimes, when we could get some gasoline, we covered our hands, necks and even our faces with it, to avoid being bitten by them.

During the day we also suffered from mosquitoes: bigger ones; the enemy helicopters. The problem with the enemy helicopters was that they could fire missiles from a great distance. Sometimes we could see them, on the horizon. They just looked like insects. We had no idea that they were very dangerous, until several times, out of the blue, our armoured cars or canons were hit by their missiles.

One morning we were told that, the next day, some of our tanks and infantry units were going to attack Iraq's army. We were so excited. We thought we would soon be pushing their army back. We were so stupid; we didn't know this war would go on for another eight years.

Very early in the morning, the operation started. When our tanks were about to pass us, we switched our radio transmitter onto the same channel as theirs, so we could listen to their conversations. Very soon, we realised that the operation was failing. We heard the commander of one tank asking about the other tanks, and a voice responded, saying, 'tanks 3, 4, 6, 8...' and then a code word which we knew meant 'destroyed'.

Only hours before the operation, we had spoken to some of the tank personnel. We were talking about their worst fears, and one of them said: 'Dying inside a tank is tough. If we get hit by an enemy missile, if we're lucky the shells inside the tank will explode. That way at least we'll die quickly. But if a missile jams the tank door and sets it on fire, that's a slow and painful death. Basically, we'd be barbecued'.

The last words of the person in that tank were painful and heart-breaking. One agonised groan and then we lost radio communication. He must been burning alive.

We were placed for a while in a big army base in Ahwas, a town in the south of Iran. The town was under fire from the canons of Iraq's army. The fear of death was palpable everywhere. For the first time we really understood the horrific meaning of being under fire from shells and bullets. One day, when one of the units needed to take some ammunition from the stores, part of the ammunition caught fire and began to explode. I still don't know how the fire started. There were different rumours; some people believed it was the work of spies, some people believed it happened because of Iraq's shelling and some people believed it happened because of safety failures. As I said before, that army base was huge and there were lots of tanks, canons and ammunition stores. The fire started with small calibre bullets, and we heard a series of explosions. We were told that some special unit was trying to deal with it and were ordered to go to the shelters. I and two of my good friends went to a small shelter which was dug into the ground, and for more security we covered our heads with a piece of wood. By covering our heads with that wood we became unable to see anything outside our shelter. We could just hear the sound of explosions. The noise of bullets was terrifying, but we were hoping that the fire and explosions would be brought under control soon. Inside that little shelter we started to eat some food, from time to time making jokes and laughing, typical of the behaviour of army personnel. One of my friends told me: 'Hey, you like films! So you must like all these explosions. It's like we are in a western or a war film, and the characters are shooting at each other!'

Sometime later, the explosions got more severe, but we were still joking around. Suddenly, there was a huge bang, and a further wave of them thumped our heads against the wall of our shelter. We noticed lots of debris raining onto our shelter and its surroundings. One of my friends moved the wood a little bit, looked outside and said, astonished: 'There's nobody around! Where is everybody?' We all looked outside, but we couldn't see anybody else. Again, another massive explosion, which shook all of us. We knew that with this going on we could not be safe in that little shelter, so we immediately started to run to the other side the of base. After several hundred metres we stopped, because we thought that was a safe distance from the source of the explosion. But again, a massive explosion shook the ground like a big earthquake. So we carried on running. This happened several more times. We still weren't far enough away to be safe. We didn't know what to do. On the one hand, the explosions were getting bigger, and there was not a single person in the entire huge base to tell us what to do. On the other hand we thought, as army personnel, we shouldn't flee the base without orders to do so. We had such a ridiculous sense of duty. While we were in that little shelter, cracking jokes, the rest of the troops had been ordered to evacuate the base, but we hadn't noticed.

Eventually, we got right to the other side of the base. By now, we thought surely we were far enough away, but we were wrong. The explosions were so severe, we couldn't even stay there. Outside the base there was an embankment where we thought we would be safe. We passed through the barbed wire fence with great difficulty and got to the embankment. From there we could see part of the town. People were evacuating it, greatly worried and frightened. Ordinary people didn't know what was happening; they thought the Iraqi army was bombing the town and was very close to occupying it. For some time we stayed on that embankment, still thinking that we shouldn't completely abandon the base, and should remain close to it. Suddenly we saw a massive sheet of flame inside the base, covering a huge area to a height of 20 or 30 meters. Immediately after that, the terrifying sounds of a massive wave of explosions threw us several metres away. I had never seen such a huge fire or explosion in my life, not even in those Hollywood war films. For some time, we lay on the ground in a state of shock. Our surroundings looked like the depths of hell. The smell of gunpowder filled our noses and mouths and dust covered our faces and bodies. When we recovered and found ourselves just shocked and bruised, we got up and ran with all our energy. When we reached the town only a few people were still there. The rest had left their houses and work places. And the roads out of the town were still full of cars and people escaping.

Even after many more years of war and other difficult situations, I never saw or experienced such overwhelming fear among the people of any town. We too got on that road to escape. Now it was afternoon and we could still hear the explosions. Several miles outside the town, we saw a police station. We decided to go and stay there, but thought it better to wait awhile, hoping that the explosions would stop and we could go back to our base. We were also hesitant because these places had a very bad reputation. Corruption and bribery were common practice in most of them. However we didn't have any other choice: because we were military and it was a military base, we had to stay there. First we sat on the other side of the road, to rest and kill more time. The road was very busy with frightened people trying to escape. While we were sitting there, we noticed some bare-footed children playing close to the road. There was a small pothole full of dirty water and the children had brought little boxes and cans to play with that water and mix it with the dust. Those were their toys. We looked at them and their play. In that big dry desert, that hole with its puddle of dirty water was like a sea for them, and they were playing as if they were at the seaside.

After a few minutes, a little girl came up to us. She had a gold-coloured necklace and bare feet, with a gold-coloured chain tied around one of her ankles, and she carried a can full of dirty water. The little girl was staring at us with a beautiful smile, and in wonder. Maybe she was surprised at the way we looked and our general condition. Our faces and clothes were covered with dust; we must have looked ridiculous. For some time she stared at us until I smiled and asked: 'Hey, little girl, what is your name?' But she didn't answer; maybe she didn't understand what I was saying. I asked her the same question again, but she was still looking at us with her beautiful smile and didn't answer. One of my friends said: 'These children are either gypsies or belong to an Arab minority tribe. That's why she doesn't understand what you're saying'. Minutes later a little boy with dark skin came close to her, and he too stared at us with surprise. Now, in their faces I could see a sad fellow-feeling and pity. They could feel that we must have had a very bad day. I really wanted to talk to them. I wanted to ask them in the language of innocence:
Black boy, what is mixed with your blood?
I have the waters of the sea, sir.
You sad bare-chested girl, what do you sell?
I am selling the waters of the sea, sir. (1)

These children didn't know what was going on, and were looking at our pitiful situation compassionately. After all that fear and madness, we found ourselves surrounded by the purity and innocence of children. These children brought the splendour of life to the abyss of hell. When we finally went to the police station, as we had anticipated, they weren't helpful at all. They didn't give us any food, or even a blanket. They asked us to go to the yard and stay there for the night. We were sitting in the corner of the yard when we suddenly heard some people mourning in a strange and unfamiliar way. We went back to the building to find out what was going on. It seemed that a while earlier, a lorry had lost control, left the road and killed two children. Its terrified driver had wanted to escape the war, but his fear of death had resulted in more death. When we got there several police officers had already wrapped the children's bodies in blankets, and some men and women from their family were crying and mourning. The police asked us to return to the yard, but before we left I looked over at one of the blanket-wrapped bodies and saw something sticking out of it. A little dusty foot, and around the ankle a gold coloured chain.

No it wasn't her, it could not be her. Such innocence and beauty should not be killed like that. She hadn't even seen a real sea yet. Was the other one that dark boy? I didn't want to believe it.

Wrapped in our sorrow, we went back to the yard and lay down on the ground. The ground was still hot. Now stars were appearing in the sky. We could hear a mother's anguished voice crying constantly. She was mourning in a special way; calling out words we couldn't understand, but we knew it was the voice of profound sadness and loss. Now fear of the day merged into a dark and sad night. I wanted to ask that mother in the language of pain and sorrow:
Where do these salt tears come from, mother?
I am weeping the waters of the sea, sir. (2)

For some time I looked at the sky. I saw the dark night mourning its stars. I asked the dark night:
What is the source of the endless bitterness of my heart?
The waters of the sea are extremely bitter, sir. (3)

I remember another shocking event during the war between Iran and Iraq. Also during the time I was at the Army University, we heard that the Iranian forces had launched a massive attack. They managed to recapture a large area in a desert south of Iran. Several days later all the students were brought to that area to see the Iranians' victory and get the valuable experience for their future career. The desert was full of the dead bodies of Iraqi forces. Dead bodies under hot sun develop a uniquely horrible smell. These bodies were like balloons waiting to be punctured. Mosquitoes and other insects were gathering close to their eyes and mouths and eating them.

We saw groups of 20 or 30 or more... the dead bodies of Iraqi soldiers were spread across the desert. They were the prisoners that were executed. The Iranian forces got that so-called victory by executing hundreds or thousands of Iraqi prisoners. The faces and behaviour of those who were involved and still alive in that battle ground and massacre were much more disturbing than these dead bodies. Years later when I escaped to Iraq I found that Iraqis had named the day 'Prisoners' Day'. That was to commemorate the execution of lots of prisoners by Iranian forces.

I also remember my duties when I was sent to Kurdistan, in particular the tragic death of a horse. It was early morning on a summer's day. I woke up to the sunrise and a beautiful view of mountains and their green foothills. To clear my mind from its darkness and lassitude, I lit up a cigarette. It would poison my body and pollute my beautiful surroundings, but I thought the damage caused by a cigarette was very little in comparison with that of my job. I was a young Iranian army officer, in charge of a small base with nearly eighty personnel in the middle of a Kurdish village. It was a job I hated.

The villagers were already awake and some of them were working on their land. For a while I just looked at the immense and beautiful mountain and whispered: 'Hey mountain, do you know how much I hate my job and my uniform?' I was supposed to be protector of these poor villagers. From whom? From counter-revolutionaries, against Saddam Hussein's army, various criminals...but in reality we ourselves were acting as oppressors.

A couple of hours later, my commander asked me to go to the main base to see him. I was supposed to be his deputy, and he was responsible for our unit, but this motherfucker left me with almost all members of the unit in our base, and himself stayed in the main base which was much more secure, with lots of good facilities. On our way I saw several big lorries carrying mules and horses. That meant there was going to be an operation, either against the opposition or the Iraqi army. Horses and mules were used to carry ammunition and army equipment through the mountains. I looked at the beautiful eyes of the horses and thought, 'Even these beautiful animals have to pay the price for our madness.'

We were close to the main base when, suddenly Iraqi fighter jets appeared overhead, and anti-aircraft weapons started shooting inside the main base. The Iraqis must have seen the animal transport, and knew the Iranians were preparing for attack. After several minutes of gunfire and several massive explosions, the Iraqi fighter jets flew off and the situation calmed down. Eventually all the cars and lorries got inside the base, and we realised that the bombs had destroyed several air-raid shelters, and one building where people had been working. The smell of death and blood was everywhere.

16

I got out of the car and walked to the other side of the base. I sat next to a tree in a corner, and lit up a cigarette. Several minutes later, some soldiers came along, with horses and mules. They were tying the animals to wooden posts when suddenly the anti-aircraft guns started to shoot again. Two horses hadn't been tied up yet, and when the shooting started they bolted. The soldiers with them ran to the shelters. One of the loose horses had stopped next to a building, but the other one ran in the opposite direction. She tried to get past a roll of barbed wire, but her legs and body got caught up in it. Although I was terrified by this new bombardment, I said to myself: 'Fuck it; I am not going into these shelters, still full of blood and death.' I decided to go and get the horse that was tangled in the barbed wire.

As I went towards it, a soldier came out of a shelter and shouted: 'Be careful, sir, there's a minefield over there,' and immediately ran back inside. I didn't know what to do; on the one hand I was afraid, but on the other, the poor horse's legs and stomach were bleeding. I didn't want to get too close to her because she might have moved away from me and closer to the minefield. I said: 'Hey, beautiful horse, calm down, don't move...' But I couldn't hear my own voice for the roar of the guns.

The horse tried with all her energy to release herself again. She managed to move a couple of steps forward and almost got free, but suddenly one of her hooves stepped on an anti-personnel mine. I had to throw myself to the ground because the explosion had thrown debris and stones around. When I found out I wasn't injured, I looked up at the horse. One of her hooves was crushed, the bone of the same leg was pulverised up to the knee, and part of her neck and body were bleeding. She was shivering all over, but I couldn't find any fear or pain in her face. Horses definitely handle their fear and pain differently.

Hopelessly, I tried to calm her down: 'Don't move, stay there...' Why did I think that beautiful horse, in that situation, could hear or understand me? A moment later she moved again, put her hooves on two more mines, and collapsed to the ground. Now I could just see her head and neck. Where I lay, they were level with me. Several times she calmly shook her head, as if approaching the end of her struggle. That was all; then it was finished, and she was dead, with open eyes. I had already witnessed the death and injury of lots of humans, but now for the first time I saw how a horse dies. I didn't hear any screaming, I couldn't see any pain on her face; it was just like the end of a magnificent dance; dance of death.

Back at the base, I had to check the guards to make sure that they didn't do anything stupid: do not go to sleep, do not shoot, do not smoke at your post... the usual bullshit, but if I hadn't said it every night, I knew that somebody would start shooting out of fear or stupidity: 'Oh sir, I am sure I saw some shadows with guns, I heard voices, I though we'd been invaded...'

Eventually, I got to my own shelter, and finally had a chance to take off my boots and put my gun away. I didn't have any appetite, but I had to eat something because my stomach was painful and acidic. I ate some cold food, lit up a cigarette and switched on the TV. We had several TVs on our base, and one of them was in my shelter. Although we were not allowed to watch Iraqi channels, everybody watched them. They were full of propaganda, but at least they showed some music and films. There was a film on one of Iraqi channels. My eyes were on the screen, but my mind was miles away and full of sadness. Suddenly I became aware of some Spanish dancing in the scene I was gazing at. That poetic dance and music were supposed to bring happiness and exhilaration to the viewer, but had quite the opposite effect on me. It reminded me of that horse, and her dance of death. I was close to tears, but I had to stop myself. I was supposed to be a tough commander. No, I wasn't allowed to cry; not for the villagers, not for the soldiers, not for myself, and not even for a horse.

When I'd had enough, I escaped with my friend Seerous. We had to hide for several months before we managed to escape into Kurdistan, where Seerous joined an opposition group. By that time I had spent five years at war and several months as a fugitive. I was so tired that I just wanted to find a way to go somewhere that I could live peacefully. Although Seerous had had a similar experience to me, even harsher in some respects, he still wanted to carry on and fight against the dictators: he was still thirsty and full of passion for freedom. Whether or not I agreed with his chosen path, he was much more serious and determined than me to fight against Iran's Islamic regime. This is an honest confession. I was tired and looking for a peaceful life somewhere else, but he wanted to carry on fighting. I entered Iraqi territory, out of desperation and under the illusion – fed by Iraq's propaganda machine-that they would help people like me to go to another country.

In the beginning when I introduced myself and told them that I was an Iranian officer and had escaped from the army because I didn't want to fight against them, they were very hospitable. Smiles and appreciation were the order of the day. Even during my first interrogation at an army base close to the border, they asked me which country in Europe I would like to go to (fucking jokers). Hospitality was over very shortly. I was transferred from that army base to a detention camp in another army base in a town called Karkok, where I met several other Iranians. Three of them were very young, and had also come to Iraq hoping to go to Europe. But we started to realise that there was something wrong. If as the Iraqis said we were their guests, why had they kept us in detention? One week later, I was told to get ready to go to Baghdad. They took me to a prison under the authority of Mokhaberat, their secret service. They handed me over to several military guards at one of the prison gates. I didn't know where I was until one of the guards brought a blindfold and tried to put it on my eyes, but there was something wrong with it and it didn't fit on my face and eyes. They asked me to take off my t-shirt, and then covered my face and eyes with that. At that point I realised they were taking me to prison. They took me to a car and although I couldn't see anything, I was told to put my head on my knees. It was a very scary time. I thought they are going to torture me, but why? Maybe they think I am an Iranian spy.

Sometime later the car stopped and they took me to a building and put me in a cell. They asked me to remove my t-shirt from my eyes and than left. I looked at my cell which was seven by eight meters in size, with two dirty blankets. From the very beginning I could hear some noises from the other cells. Several hours later a guard opened the door of my cell and asked me to go with him. For the first time I saw several cells along a corridor. These cells seemed to be full of prisoners. I wished they had put me with the other prisoners; being alone in a cell is very difficult. I entered an office where an Iraqi officer was waiting for me with an interpreter and a big smile. The Iraqi officer shook my hand and asked the interpreter to tell me that I shouldn't be anxious, this was part of a normal and routine process, and that I would be free soon. Surely he could read the fear and disbelief on my face. Again I went through interrogation, with more or less the same repeated questions. I told them that I was just a junior officer and had left the army months ago, and that I had no idea where my unit was now. When my interrogation finished, I asked the officer: 'How long shall I be kept here?' he answered with a big smile: 'Very soon you will be free'. But this motherfucker was lying. I was in that cell alone nearly two months.

One of the worst things about that cell was that I could hear the wailing of other prisoners when they were tortured. I still remember vividly the coldness of the walls of my cell when I put my head and ears against them to listen to other prisoners suffering. It was very severe mental torture for me. Every time somebody came to my door I thought: 'Now it's my turn to be tortured'. Every time they took me out to go to the toilet, I could see the terrible condition of the other prisoners. Some of them lay down on the floor soaked in their own blood. Some of them were Iranian soldiers who had been captured in the war, and some of them were seriously injured.

Once the same Iraqi officer with the big smile came to me and said they were happy to arrange an interview on TV for me. When I was in Iran I heard lots of Iranians who managed to escape and go to Iraq were interviewed on radio or TV. More important and high profile people were interviewed on TV.

Apart from fear that my situation would get worse if I said no, I agreed to do the interview for two other reasons. First, somebody might see me on TV and let my family know that I was alive, and secondly, since all opposition groups were using these facilities- radio and TV- to send their messages to Iranian people, I too could do that and at least show my opposition to the war. After all, I told myself, 'Hip hip hooray, I am a fucking important person, that's why they want me on TV. Even in prison I am a fucking popular person!'

During my time in that cell, on a couple of occasions they brought Iranian soldiers to my cell for one or two days, and then took them away. The soldiers also pretended to be refugees, but I never saw them again. If they were refugees I would have seen them in the refugee camp. Maybe they were working for the Iraqis and this was a way to get more information out of me, or maybe they were killed by the Iraqis. One day towards the end of my time in that cell, when I was talking to one of those Iranian inmates, suddenly some noises like radio waves came from our cell's ceiling; probably something faulty had occurred in their equipment. Our cell was bugged and the prison authorities were watching us. From that moment the concept of big brother took a hold on my mind.

Iraq's authorities were hoping that by putting systematic pressure on the refugees they could make them work for them. In my final interrogation in that prison, one of the Iraqi officers asked me if I wanted to work for them. I told him: 'No, I just came here to go to another country'.

There was a guard in prison who, unlike other guards, was wearing civilian clothes. I think he was an expert torturer. Several times I recognised his voice when he was shouting and torturing other prisoners. From the first time that I met him I could feel that he hated me and was just waiting for the order of his superiors to start torturing me. After being two months in that cell I started to nag and complain about my condition. Each time I complained he would come and see me and like an addict who can see the drug before his eyes but cannot use it, would ask me angrily – but with a veneer of politeness – to calm down. On the last day of my time in that cell, he came to me with a big smile on his face and said: 'Get ready; you are going to a nice place!'

I looked at him and said to myself: 'The fucking torturer can smile too'. This motherfucker knew where I was being sent.

I was transported from one extreme to another, from the loneliness of my cell in Baghdad to an extremely overcrowded cell in Romadyeh. It was unbelievable. In a 10x10 meter cell with a toilet at the end of it, lots of prisoners were trapped. Some prisoners who had been there for a long time had their own space close to the walls and had spread out blankets. That was their territory; they didn't let anyone put a finger on their space and blanket. The only space for newcomers was a narrow corridor in the middle of the cell. There wasn't even space to stand on one foot. Prisoners were piled up on top of each other, we could hardly breathe. I saw these Iranian youngsters whom I had met at the time of my entry to Iraq. They looked extremely sad and tired. I asked them: 'Have you been here for the last two months?' They said: 'No, after only one week we were transferred to a refugee camp.' They attempted to escape, but were captured by the Iraqis and brought here. They were very young and in that cell which was full of criminals also had to survive. Sexual harassment was common. The toilet was open during the day only and was locked at night. Because of lack of space, even that toilet was occupied by several prisoners during the day, and sometimes if we needed the toilet we had to do it in front of others – fucking friendly! Atmosphere – at night these prisoners who were there for long time had a small container to piss in if they needed, but we in that narrow corridor on top of each other didn't have anything. Imagine what it was like, in that condition where we were piled up and formed a human hill, if someone had diarrhoea or had been sick. Already everyone carried lice and in that pile-up of humans the smell of dirty bodies was unbearable. Luckily there were two Kurdish brothers among the prisoners who were supportive of us. They were supporters of a Kurdish opposition group and had been in prison for several months. Because they used to live close to the border with Iran they could speak our language; Farsi. All the prisoners were afraid of them. One of them was completely mad and in order to show off and frighten the other prisoners, from time to time he slashed his hands and body with a blade. During the day these brothers would let us have a little nap on their blankets. Of course there were some long-term prisoners who would let you use their space for a little nap, but you had to pay a small price for that; money wasn't necessary, your ass or mouth was sufficient. Sexual favours could buy you temporary space to rest. During the night also we witnessed some entertainments! Some prisoners were fucking each other, as I said before it was a fucking friendly atmosphere, we had nothing to hide from each other. Eating, pissing, fucking... One midnight suddenly they threw another ten or fifteen prisoners into our cell, again those who had space didn't allow anybody to go near them, so our human pile in the middle got much bigger. A few hours later an old prisoner had a heart attack and died. So everybody started to shout and protest until the guards came to the cell and took the dead body and some prisoners out. Consigning refugees to this kind of prison before taking them to the refugee camp was part of a systematic pressure, to force them to work for them or deter them from escaping or trying to protest about their conditions. I lived like that for about a week and it was longest week of my life.

The refugee camp was just a massive desert. There was a police station at the entrance and then a huge desert. After being in that prison, I was so happy to see that huge and dirty desert. So I didn't have to be close to anyone and be fucking cuddly with any dirty and smelly body. First they took me to the police station and after some paperwork someone gave me a tent and said: 'Can you see this desert? Go and set up your tent wherever you want'.

There were many thousands of Iranian Kurds living there. They came from several tribes who used to live in the mountains on the Iran-Iraq border, but when Iraq invaded Iran they were forced to move down into the desert. The majority of them used to live in primitive conditions in Iran with no electricity or car or formal education. I was an Iranian myself but I didn't know there were so many people who lived in such a primitive state. But these tribes had been living in that desert for several years and had experienced having electricity, TV, radio...etc. Most of them were very nice people and had great sympathy for refugees like me, and for those who had left their families and ended up there. Iraq also managed to hire some of them to go to Iran for acts of sabotage and to bomb the cities, and also some of them were hired by the Iraqi authorities as human hunters. Their job was to capture any Iranian soldier and sell them to the Iraqis. The price for an officer or a member of the Iranian authorities was higher than for an ordinary soldier. In some instances they were bringing Iranian people into Iraq who wanted to be refugees, and selling them to the Iraqis. I met some Iranians in the camp who told me that smugglers were human hunters who not only got the money from the refugees but also sold them to the Iraqis, and that they had had great difficulty in convincing the Iraqis that they were refugees and had come there voluntarily. Apart from these tribes, there were some political refugees there. When I got my tent and entered the camp some of them came to help me, and brief me more about the camp. When I first met some the other refugees in the camp, one of them asked with a smile: 'How are your ass and mouth?' I didn't get what he was trying to say at the beginning. He continued and said: 'Have you been in prison?'

'Yes, I was'.

'I came out of that prison with an ass problem,' and then pointed at his friend and said: 'But he developed a mouth problem.' He was just joking about sexual abuse in the prison. I don't think any of us who spent time there can ever forget the horror. Someone else said: 'When I was there a film director was also there, and one day five prisoners asked him to play a scene in the toilet. He told them four people would be enough for the scene, but the prisoners insisted there should be five. Anyway they went to the toilet and several minutes later, the director came out shouting: "You are just fucking farmers". He came and sat next to me and said, "I told them that only four people are required, but they are just fucking ignorant. Do you know what happened? One of them put his dick in my ass, the other one in my mouth, and at the same time I had to grab and massage two other dicks with my hands. In the middle of the scene the fifth person suddenly started to hit me and asked me to make a noise like a donkey or horse. I asked him how on earth with this dick in my mouth could I make the sound of a donkey or horse. They are just farmers who used to rape their animals. They don't know anything about the art of playing a scene, fucking amateurs!"' Yes, it's true. By making things into a joke we tried to escape the harshness of reality. It wss part of our defence mechanism.

23

The camp was like a big slum and people had made rooms and shelters out of mud. Because there was no sewage system, everywhere was full of dirty water and rubbish. There was a small market, a coffee shop and bakery run by tribes-people. Every month we received a small amount of money for subsistence. I got together with some other refugees, sold our tents and bought a 4x4 meter room made of mud. We also had a little shower, which was both funny and very dangerous. Almost every day it gave us electric shocks. We had a barrel filled with water that was connected directly to high voltage overhead cables by a wire. It was very dangerous and unsafe. But there was no rule of law in that dirty slum. Several times we even heard somebody got killed or a man killed his wife, but the Iraqi police didn't give a toss about these things, they only took action if something created a problem for them, posed a threat to Iraqi security or was a political protestor.

One day after nearly a month, representatives of the Red Cross or the UN came to the camp and said that there wasn't much chance that they'd be able to help us to go to other countries. Desperation, despair and suicide were common among the refugees. Some of them tried to escape but most of them were recaptured and put in prison again, before they were brought back to camp. We never heard about the fate of some of the escapees, they just vanished; possibly they were killed by the Iraqis.

After about six months living there we heard about another refugee camp in a place called Helleh, with much better living conditions. So some political refugees organized a petition which they presented to the Romadyeh council. Eventually the Iraqis agreed to take political refugees to Helleh. The facilities there were much better. It was a camp that used to house the French industrial workers who left Iraq when the war started. Although the facilities were much better there was still no hope of leaving that country and we were still very fearful about our future. We didn't know what would happen to us if the war between Iran and Iraq ended. We were all too well aware that some Iranians were working for the Iraqi police and secret services. There was an Iranian refugee called Ali. His nickname was 'Ali Bomby'. The Iraqis gave him a car, lots of money and he was allowed to travel all over Iraq. Whenever he disappeared for some time, we knew he had gone to Iran to plant bombs in public places. The Iraqis deliberately kept him living with the rest of the refugees to encourage more of us to work for the Iraqi authorities. Anyway Ali Bomby was captured by Iranian forces on one of his missions and hanged.

After about one year of living in refugee camps in Iraq I reached the state where I thought I had nothing to lose. If I was supposed to live in that hopeless camp and die day by day, I might as well go back to Kurdistan again and join a group and fight against these killers. Already some political refugees had asked the Iraqis to let us meet and go to our political groups. I still had no idea about or knowledge of these political groups and their ideologies. I just wanted to get out of those bloody camps. Eventually I got in touch with a Marxist group and found myself on the way back to Kurdistan. I had gone to Iraq in the hope of finding a peaceful place to live, but instead I had faced prison and the disgusting camps.

So there I was, still alive, but who knew for how much longer? I learned that Seerous had been killed just a few months earlier by the Iranians. I knew from experience that if I was asked by Central Committee members to write my autobiography, this wasn't meant to celebrate my life; it would be out of suspicion. For me, answering more questions about myself made the Hell of that place complete.

Event: It was a sunny day towards the end of summer. While I was out of the shelter during the shelling, I watched as a shell landed close to a donkey that was carrying a man. The donkey died immediately and its rider, one of the brothers of the coffee shop owner, was badly injured. The next day the sun continued to shine, with no further shelling. Iraq had supplied us with some food, but everybody wanted more and better food. Local people, gathering around the dead donkey, were surprised to see that one of its legs was missing. One of them said: 'It must be the work of wolves or wild dogs.' But another responded: 'No take a good look: can't you see how cleanly the leg has been removed? A knife must have done this. Who could do such a thing?' Because of their culture and religion they had never eaten donkey's meat and they couldn't imagine who would have cut the leg off. In the afternoon of the same day, I noticed members of another political group having a barbecue, and for the sake of the local people, they were pretending that they were barbecuing lamb.

There was a little stream close to our base, with lots of frogs living around the water. One day, some of our members who had caught and killed several of these frogs were preparing them for the barbecue, but when the local people saw what was happening, they came to us very surprised and wanted to know what we were doing. How could we admit we were going to eat the frogs? One of our members came up with a good excuse: 'We are doing an autopsy in the aid of science and medical research.' On several occasions we ate snakes as well. They tasted like fish.

Weather: As the days and nights got cooler, with constant wind, it became difficult to keep warm, even in the tents. The shelling never ceased and for us, living in tents without protection was very dangerous.

Activity: We were used to living in tents, and each one of us had a sleeping bag and blanket. But tents could not protect us from shelling and its deadly debris. In order to be safe and more comfortable, we decided to build a couple of rooms out of stone. Even with the coffee shop brothers and three or four local people who assisted us, this was a difficult job. We had to cut trees to make roofs, and gather lots of stones. The work went more quickly after one of the locals offered his son Ali and his donkey to help move the stones.

Entertainment: Ali was a young man who had a learning disability caused by mental illness, and because of that he was a prime target for some of the more cruel locals and smugglers to taunt and laugh. While we were building the rooms, Ali and his donkey gathered stones and brought them to us. During a break, one man said: 'Hey Ali, did you notice when you put stones on the back of your donkey his balls tighten up and when you remove the stones, his balls are free and dangling?' It was true. Poor Ali, with a big grin on his face, first put some stones on the back of his donkey, then removed them, and in the meantime kept checking his donkey's balls and laughing crazily at his discovery about the relationship between the weight and the donkey's balls.

Gossip: when Ali and his donkey had left, a man told us that Ali was in charge of two donkeys, one male and one female, and that he had sexual relations with the female. One time when the boy wanted to have sex with her, the male donkey became very jealous and attacked him, kicking his head. That's how Ali's brain was damaged, said the man.

Leisure Time: I remember when we got a chance to play football against members of another political party who had flat land close to their base which was suitable for a game. We played twice, winning the first time, and then in the middle of the second match the shelling started, so we had to stop. We set the time for another game the next day, but the play was delayed, luckily for us, because five or six minutes after we were due to start a shell landed in the middle of the pitch! Spies must have found out that we were playing football there and had informed the Iranian authorities.

Weather: Snow everywhere. This reduced the danger of ground attacks, at least, because it blocked all the roads, but shelling continued and we were fed up with the constant wind, which was getting on our nerves because we couldn't hear the noise of shells properly and it made our situation even more dangerous.

Health Service: Not having had a shower in about a month, I was hoping that it wouldn't be more than another two months before the shelling stopped for long enough to give me a chance, but every time I mentioned this, the others begged me not to shower, joking that whenever I tried, the shelling started up again.

Event: One snowy and cold day, we heard an explosion followed by the moans of those who had been hit. It turned out that the well-known leader of a party next to us had been badly injured. Not long before this he had asked someone to bring him a book from a library inside Iran, but the secret service had heard about it, and booby-trapped the book so that as soon as he opened it a small quantity of explosive material was detonated. The resulting explosion had severed both his hands, blinding him as well.

Hopes: Of the revolutionary: to bring about the dictator's downfall. Of the ordinary people: to get food, doctors, hospitals, schools and security. Of the smugglers: to pay less to the authorities of both countries (major parties in that region were charging smugglers a percentage): not to be captured or wounded by a mine. Of the spies: to be promoted by the authorities and thus get more money. Of the double agents: the possibility of working for both major parties as well, because they seemed to have lots of money. Of Ali: to have more donkeys. Of Ali's donkeys: to carry less weight.

Hates and fears: Revolutionaries: spies, torturers, the authorities and being criticised. Ordinary people: poverty, war and dictatorship. Smugglers: mines, and paying a percentage of their profit to all the different authorities. Spies: being captured. Ali's donkeys: Ali.

Weather: As the snow began to melt, the paths and the road became passable again, making it less dangerous to travel, but the danger of ground attack increased.

Event: In response to the news that large numbers of Iranian forces were gathering on the border with Iraq, an Iraqi fighter jet bombarded the mountains around us with chemical gas. This was a psychological attack, as well; they wanted to deter Iran from an invasion that was becoming more imminent.

Activities: Apart from trying to find out the latest situation inside Iran, we had to look after groups of mothers who were approaching us daily to learn the whereabouts of their sons and daughters among the various political groups. Some of them managed to come secretly, but many were forced by the Iranian authorities to convince their children to stop fighting and return to Iran. In that region there were two main Iranian opposition parties with substantial numbers of supporters and members, but these parties, unfortunately, were fighting against each other. One of them was stationed very close to us and had much better facilities, but they refused to look after those mothers whose children belonged to the other party (sectarianism at its best!), so these mothers came to us instead. Due to constant shelling and very real dangers, our group had been reduced to no more than six members, the others having been moved to other bases. So not only did the six of us have to resist daily shelling, and to guard our base; we were expected, as well, to look after these tired and terrified mothers. All of us were worn out.

Leisure time: One sunny and beautiful day before the shelling had started and when, for a change, we had no guests to care for, I decided to get a book and climb to the top of a nearby mountain to read and relax. Several minutes after sitting down to enjoy the book I heard some low but sharp noises. At first I thought there were a few bees flying around my head, and then suddenly a stone exploded next to my ear. Someone was shooting at me! I rushed downhill to the hamlet's coffee shop to tell one of its owners what had happened. He told me that my 'resting place' was where the Iraqi opposition went to watch the Iraqi army. 'The Iraqis must have learned about this, which is why they were shooting at you,' he said: 'Your head and shoulders would have stood out clearly above the horizon, an ideal target for their snipers. You are very lucky to be alive.' He gave me a glass of tea and while I was drinking it, I noticed an old lady with gold teeth and tattoos on her face and hands sitting and smoking a kalian, our name for a hubble-bubble.

It was unusual to see any women there, no matter how old. Talking to her and smiling in a familiar way as if they knew her well, were some of the smugglers, their faces sly.

Later, the owner of the coffee shop explained that she was a pimp, nicknamed Madam Biscuit by the men who went to her place; because they paid in biscuits as well as cash for the women she was in charge of. The smuggling business was creating all sorts of pleasurable job opportunities, it seemed. Even during wartime and under fire.

Weather: Getting warmer but still windy.

Hopes: Medical staff: That they could stitch up the fat ass whose constant farting was the cause of this wind! Madam Biscuit: more biscuits.

Gossip: One of our medical staff has been seen buying lots of biscuits. Ali has been attacked by his donkey again.

True stories: Our base was a very good place to meet other people who had suffered harsh and unbelievable experiences and hear from political activists - those with different ideologies and beliefs from our own - the almost unimaginable stories of how they, their families and friends had suffered prison and torture. To watch the hardship ordinary people were going through in their struggle for a decent life was both sad, and at the same time inspiring.

Health service: Eventually I decided to have a shower. It was a good sunny day and the shelling hadn't started yet. It had become essential to wash myself now, because the bloody lice were eating up my body. We had a barrel that had to be filled with water first, and the shower consisted of a small cabinet with walls of cloth and plastic. Needless to say, such walls couldn't protect us from shellfire. This encouraged us to wash very quickly and hope that no shell would land close to the shower.

Wankcuted : (Dear readers, please do not look this word up in any dictionary because you will not find it. It is my own contribution to the English language.) : As I knew from experience that the shelling could start up again soon, I washed myself very fast, but before I put my clothes back on, I thought that since there was no shelling, it would be a great opportunity for a wank. This was not because I was horny (how could anybody be in our situation!) I just wanted to know if I was still a man! In other words: could I get it up? After months in this place, was I still okay in that department? So here goes: start by massaging it – you know what I mean by 'it' – but be quick, because along with the massage, I needed a lot of imagination. Imagine what, though? Shelling? The next explosion? Injury? Possible death? What? Come on man, concentrate! Think of something sexy! But what? Ali's donkey? Oh, don't be disgusting! What else? For months I haven't seen or felt anything sexy- Hurry up! Shelling may start soon! What about Madam Biscuit? She is very old, but she could be sexy, I guess. Don't even think about her! I wish the revolutionary morality would allow me to buy some biscuits and give them to her. What else? Months ago I had the chance to watch a TV film with a sex scene in it, so try to concentrate on it. Immediately, though, I remember other scenes from that film, a propaganda film showing lots of dead bodies of soldiers in the desert. Damn, what else? Don't know, hurry up, just massage it faster, maybe with the help of heat or friction I'll manage to succeed, faster, faster, oh my God I think it is waking up! Thanks God, this is very good news for me, yes, I can still get it up, hooray…but I have to be faster, come on, you can do it.

Suddenly, in the middle of my struggle, a shell landed close to the shower and I could feel its debris flying all around me. For seconds I froze. The shock ran right through my body. That was it, I was wankuted.

We were surrounded by beautiful nature, but far from human nature. We were forced and restricted to suppress our feelings and natural way of living.

Hopes: Revolutionary: with people's help we can defeat these torturers. Ordinary people: food, jobs, happiness. Smugglers: that the war could continue because their business was booming. Spies: more money and one day to be celebrated as a 007. Ali: to have more donkeys. Madam Biscuit: to have biscuits with cream! Medical staff: to look after Madam Biscuit's ladies.

Gossip: Iran's army is going to attack this area soon. Iraq's army is going to use chemical weapons. Chemical Ali – the nickname of an Iraqi officer who was responsible for other chemical attacks - has been seen in the area. One of our medical staff keeps buying biscuits. Ali has been attacked again, this time by both of his donkeys.

Hates: Everybody hates chemical bombs except chemical Ali. The Kurdish people have a bitter memory of being bombarded by Iraq's forces. In a place called Halabch many people were killed by Iraqi chemical bombs.

During the war between Iran and Iraq, the Iraqis deployed chemical weapons many times. This is not only a weapon of mass destruction, but also an extremely cruel way of killing humans, animals and destroying nature. Lucky survivors - if you call them lucky - of chemical attacks have to carry painful injuries to their body and mind for the rest of their lives.

Event: Eventually one of our medical staff admitted that he used his own injection (you know what I mean) on one of Madam Biscuit's ladies! It was against the rules and he was betraying the morality expected of revolutionaries. By admitting what he'd done, he knew he could not remain with us or even in the area, so he decided to go to the Iraqi refugee camp. I felt I had to tell him how harsh and disgusting the prisons and camps in Iraq were. I was an expert on this, having spent a year in these places previously. 'They can't be worse than this,' he said to me. 'We die a hundred times every day here'. Then he was gone.

Rumours and gossip: for several days shelling stopped and an opposition group announced that they had managed to kill the commander of the army units that were responsible for shelling us. Some people, though, were saying that the group had started to negotiate with the authorities, and that was the reason why shelling had stopped.

Entertainment: 'Come on and see what these bastards are doing,' a friend said one day. I could hear dogs barking and figured that some people, probably smugglers, had started watching dog fights again and gambling on the outcome. But my friend said, 'Come and look, this is unbelievable!' When we went to the place where the barking came from, I saw that the sick bastards had chained a female dog to a tree, put red paint on her head and face and were encouraging a pack of male dogs to fight over which one would have sex with that poor, terrified bitch. It was pure barbarism. I nearly threw up at the idea that so-called "humans" could do such things to animals. Moments later the shelling started again, and for the first time I was truly happy to see these shells landing. At least they ended that disgusting show.

Rumour and gossip: If the war between these countries ends, the first casualties will be the political groups, who will be handed over to their respective authorities. All political groups were supported either by Iran or Iraq, and knowing the brutal nature of both regimes, there was a great mistrust among members of the political groups towards them. We all knew they supported opposition groups because they were at war and one day, when the war was over, they could stop their support and even hand us over to our enemies.

Event: We got an addition to the 'medical staff'. Poor man, he used to live in Europe, but had come to Iran and couldn't get out again. He was more knowledgeable about medicines than the rest of our staff, but he was terrified. I couldn't blame him. He had lived in peaceful Europe for many years, and couldn't even speak Farsi properly. To be stuck in the area where we were hiding out, and in these conditions, would be a severe shock for anyone who had grown up in a more or less civilised society. It was a complete accident that he had wound up there. Not only was our way of living totally foreign to him, he didn't have the slightest motivation to fight.

Gossip: Some guy said: 'I will never ask for help from this new member of our medical staff. Why? Because in Europe, where people like him grow up, homosexuality and corruption are common. I don't trust him. The other day, I saw him giving an injection to a man, and for an injection you need only to expose a little bit of butt. But he pulled the pants of that man right down to his knees!'

Environment: Although there were always glimmers of hope - hope of reaching and getting closer to freedom, of seeing and experiencing the human struggle for a better life, of being surrounded by wild and beautiful nature with its amazing sunrises and sunsets – it was at the same time very harsh and brutal. We were far from family, in constant fear of shelling, of being arrested, poisoned, of stepping on a mine; in fear of invasion by our enemy and of death - and all this on top of years of accumulated harsh experiences weighing on our bodies and minds.

Part (2)
Real Nightmares
Caused by Harsh Environment

Nightmares: First I heard a massive explosion and then for some time I was flying like a feather. Moments later I hit the ground. I must have been hit by a shell, or maybe I stepped on a mine. First a severe shock and then absolute tranquility. Was I dead? I must have been dead. Eventually I had reached the end. I still didn't want to; I was hoping that a miracle had happened and saved me from all this horror. Oh, pain again! I felt pain in my legs, no I wasn't dead. I was tied up on a torture bed. My eyes were covered with a blindfold and someone was lashing my feet. I must have been captured and now I was in an Iranian prison. I didn't know what I should say; fear and pain wouldn't let me think. How about my friend, Seerous, Had he been arrested too? Oh no, this can't be true! I had never been in any Iranian prisons.

'You are mistaken.'

'Who are you?'

'A voice'

'Fuck off! Are you telling me that I am a madman and hear voices in my head? I know some mentally disturbed people hear voices in their heads, but not me, I am not mad.'

'No. You are having a nightmare and in nightmares you can hear and see many strange things. You are not in an Iranian prison. You have just read about the torture that goes on there or spoken to the victims. It is the power of your bloody imagination that is making you see and feel these things.'

'Are you a psychologist?'

'No, you have created me. I am in your mind and of course influenced by the environment.'

'I have created you for the sake of my story. In this way my readers can understand more about the mind of a writer.'

***

Oh, I should run faster, they are coming closer, to capture me. I am trying hard to run, but I cannot move. Try harder! Good. Now I can run. I must run faster, but my feet don't feel the ground; I am running over dead bodies. Dead bodies cover the entire land in this desert; they are everywhere, all the way to the horizon.

'You escaped from that war. You are not in that desert any more,'
The Voice said.

I must be in an Iraqi prison. I can hear the barking of wild dogs. I
open my eyes and see Ali's face, but with the ears of a donkey. He is
laughing madly, his teeth like donkey's teeth, and I have to run away
again. I have always been fit and strong. I have to run faster, I am going
to score a goal; I am going to hit that ball so hard it is sure to pass the
goalkeeper! I hit it hard, but it isn't a ball, it is a human head. I have to
run faster, this is a madhouse! Why does my mouth taste so bitter? I
vomit and part of my tongue that is covered with blood drops out. I
know I shouldn't have drunk that water, it must have been poisoned. I
have to vomit, to get rid of the poison in my stomach. Someone is
holding my hands and my sickness and pain have disappeared. I am
dead and she must be an angel, but I don't want to see an angel when I
am dead; I don't believe in Heaven or Hell. Look at that woman in the
crowd: why is she crying blood? Her tears are blood; she must have lost
her loved ones. I am crying. No, I shouldn't cry, I am in a small shelter.
Maybe it is my grave and it is me who is crying blood.
'Wake up, wake up!'
Someone pours cold water on my face and takes my blindfold
away. A man with a whip in his hand says: 'Stand up. You better walk
a bit. It's good for your feet.' Oh, I'm in the torture room again.
'No it's your madness. You read about it or hear it from victims. It's
not your story, it's theirs.' The Voice said.
'But I can feel the pain in my feet and my soul.'
'You are imagining that.'
'You'd better shut up! I've written a novel about torture in Iranian
prisons called *The Last Scene*, yet I have never been in one. Call this
creativity. I am a writer; don't tell me that I am mad.'
'Strong imagination is very close to madness: always remember
that.'
I am in a prison cell alone. I can hear many other prisoners crying.
The sound of a lash as it cuts through the air is terrifying. Now I can
hear the barking of mad dogs. Oh my God, they are coming for me!
Don't tell me that I am mad. I recognise this cell. This is my cell in the
Iraqi prison. I haven't invented it.
'You saw these dogs somewhere else. This again is your
imagination. Some of these smugglers were captured as well, but you
saw them years later. You are mixing up the times and places.'
'Yes, I do that, I am a writer. I can create what I want.'
'Just do not believe so strongly in what you have invented.'

34

'Why?'

'Because it is driving you crazy.'

I am thrown from the top of a high mountain into a valley. I can feel myself flying and I am so terrified. I think: I am going to die.

'Once again you are imagining this. You must have seen that in a film or read about it. You are mixing things up with real life.'

'Of course! I am a fiction writer!'

'No you are simply mad.'

'Keep your fucking opinion to yourself. I didn't ask for it! You must be one of these stupid people who are more interested in who is writing than what is being written. Do you want to know about the size of my dick too? Or perhaps you know already.'

Once I hanged myself from a tree. It was very painful, but the tree rescued me. When I hung from the branch, the other branches suddenly took me in their arms. I know the tranquility and calmness of trees. She rescued me.

'Again you are talking nonsense. You are mixing up real life with one of your own stories and other crazy images.' says the Voice.

'Yes, I am a writer. What do you expect?'

'Your problem is that, you imagine a story and write it down. Then you imagine yourself in the middle of that story, and then the story after that, until you get further and further away from reality. Why are you writing such things? You frighten people. They think you are crazy.'

'Who cares? Do you think if I were writing about the realities of life, I wouldn't hear all this nonsense? When people don't understand you, they invent nonsense, which I call dick theories. I think Ali's donkeys are more realistic than all of us; they are the ones forced to carry heavy weight and we just think of their balls. Anyway, I am glad that those donkeys never attacked me. I don't know why my comrades have become suspicious of me. I haven't done anything. The other day I noticed that they searched my belongings. Not only have they asked me to write my life story, but also they keep asking me strange questions. Can't they see that I've put my life on the line here? I prefer to die rather than be seen as a traitor'.

Thank God, today was sunny and hot and the shelling hadn't started yet. I was standing close to the coffee shop and I saw Madam Biscuit sitting on top of one of Ali's donkeys with Ali walking behind them and studying his donkey's balls. Strangely, the balls were touching the ground and from time to time Ali gave stones to Madam Biscuit. When they came close to me, Madam Biscuit asked me: 'Why don't you come to my place?' to which I replied: 'No, I can't, my revolutionary morality doesn't allow me to come with you. Plus I am so dirty that I need to wash myself.' She smiled. 'Come with me,' she urged. 'You don't have to do anything'.

I went with Ali and Madam Biscuit and entered a small house where there were a couple of ladies who stared at me. I didn't know what to do or say and a moment later I decided it was better to leave because I didn't want to do anything. As I was leaving I saw another lady who had wild flowers in her hand. I looked at her beautiful eyes and what I saw was splendid. In bewilderment, I went with her to the other room, but she was under the influence of opium and fell asleep before we could do anything. I just lay there, staring at her beauty.

'Hey, don't forget you are having a nightmare, not a sweet dream,' says The Voice.

'Damn! Eventually you show your true face. Even you do not want me to have a nice time.'

'There are no nice times in nightmares.'

I wasn't doing anything more than looking at her beauty, but suddenly a wind tore the clothes away from her neck and shoulders and I could see that she was covered with lice; her whole body being eaten by them. Again, there was a bitter taste in my mouth and I ran out and poked it. A part of my tongue that was covered with blood dropped out.

I have looked for you everywhere
In my dream
In lonely and winding roads
In the endless streets
In prison
In war
In exile
In the smile of flowers, the splendour of mountains, the warmness of sun
In the magic symphony of waves
I have looked for you.

I asked Fire: where is she?
'Burned in the memories of butterflies.' Burned man.
I asked Sea: where is the source of my hopes?
'Buried in the depths of oceans.' Buried man.
I asked Sun: show me the light of my life.

'It is lost in the darkness of night.' Man of darkness.
I asked God: where is my angel, then?
'In my Heaven.' Godless man.
I asked the Mirrors: where is that eternal image?
'Broken in a reflection of hopelessness.' Man of shadow.

No, I have never believed them
And now in the poor glitter of your eyes
I can see that
God has gone, the sun has disappeared in the west, the sea dried up, the fire burnt out and the mirrors broken.
     And I have believed my misery.

 Now I walk between two horizons
 The horizon of pain and the horizon of loneliness
 Illusions or hopes in front
Time and place are mixed
Exactly like a parallel world
    I'll see you tomorrow
Tomorrow was yesterday
Yesterday was the day that you went to eternity
And I can't wait to see you tomorrow
That is our life; a succession of day and night, light and darkness, hope and despair (4)

'You did it again. You keep mentioning this mysterious lady again and again. I can find similar references in your other stories. Were you ever in love with a prostitute?'

'That is exactly what I call "dick theory". This poem is my own creation and it is not your business. I am a writer with a powerful imagination, and I don't care if you call me mad. Now go and leave me alone! Go and disappear from my nightmares.'

'You want to be in charge of your own nightmares? You must be mad. Nobody can direct or control their nightmares.'

'I can, I am a writer.'

I was hungry and tired, walking in a forest of large and very tall trees. I could hardly see the tops, but I knew that up there grew the best fruits in the entire world. I wished I could reach them! Oh, I was dying of hunger! I looked at my body. It was like the bodies of those starving people in Africa. I couldn't walk any more. I lay down close to a tree and fell almost unconscious. I had decided to accept my death, so it came eventually and I was very close to the end. I knew that I was going to die alone. With my last remaining energy, I started to cry for my loneliness, but instead of tears I was crying blood. I was having a nightmare within a nightmare. No, I still wanted to live! Oh Goddess of Life and Beauty, help me, don't let me die! A moment later a miracle happened. I woke filled with energy and saw that my body was strong again – like Tarzan! My legs expanded to twice their normal size and I found I could run through the forest and with a big leap reach to the top of a tree! But when I tried to pick some fruit my legs started to deflate and I began to fall. I thought: 'This time, surely I am going to die.' Instead I landed on an ocean of flowers. Like a pop star that jumps from the stage into the arms of his supporters, the flowers caught me and with their magic scents and softness, gently put me on the ground again. Just as I was about to thank them, I noticed they were crying blood. Suddenly someone asked me in a foreign language: 'Do you remember the smell of flowers?'

'Of course,' I said.

'So you fucked them all.' he said.

'What? Are you one of the dick detectives?'

'No, but we know you visited Madam Biscuit.'

'I did not! I just had a nightmare about her.'

'But you remember the smell of posy and in your stories you wrote about the smell of flowers and bodies. We believe you to be a rapist and murderer.'

'What? I don't know what the fuck you are talking about. You'd better keep these sick, dirty thoughts to yourselves and leave me alone.'

'You'd better start to write down your autobiography.'

'Autobiography? Not again. How many times do I have to talk or write about my life? Why is it that everywhere I go people throw dirt at me? I am fed up with these suspicions. I am just a writer. Go and read all my stories. Each one is about humanity. I am not a spy, a killer or a dangerous criminal. Just leave me alone.'

***

I have a problem with my nightmares. The problem is that I remember most of them. I even write stories that are influenced and inspired by my own nightmares. I can jump from one nightmare to another and be lost in endless torment. Since I am writing about my nightmares, I need to go deep into them. Most people are lucky enough to escape their dreams when they wake up but mine are with me all the time, a constant background to my every thought and interaction.

38

'You are in another nightmare," says The Voice.

I was walking with friends in a place called 'Castle of New City'. It was a place made up of two main streets and a group of brothels. The entrance of each brothel was covered with dirty curtains and inside each room was a light that was different from anywhere else. The lights were so cruel; I could feel the human contemptuousness. Madam Biscuit was sitting in the middle of a room in a house smoking a Kalian. She said to me: 'Go to that room, she is there,' as if she knew that I was looking for someone. When I entered the room I saw Ali sitting there and drinking tea. I asked him: 'What are you doing here?' He stared at me for some time and then started to cry. He was crying blood. He said: 'One of my donkeys was killed by a land mine and the other one drank poisonous water and died. Moments later, he started to bang his head madly against the wall. I tried to calm him, but he was too crazy with grief. Soon his head and face were completely covered in blood and he said with great sadness: 'Their eyes, their eyes, I loved their eyes, but cantharides ate their eyes.' Then he left the room.

Oh, I remember writing a story called *Their Eyes*, years ago, after receiving a leaflet from Amnesty International. In that leaflet there was a picture of a young boy who had been brutally killed by criminals in Guatemala. They cut out his tongue and ears and gouged out his eyes. How could anyone do that? I remember one of my childhood nightmares. It was early morning and a worker was pushing a wagon full of dead bodies. Some of them had no eyes and some had bloody eyes that seemed to stare at me. I remember having seen that type of wagon before. Where was that? Oh, in a ghetto in Poland. I was young and strong and carrying dead bodies. All of the bodies in my wagon had eyes but were terribly thin. All of them had starved to death and I still remembered their eyes.

'Again you are mixing everything together. You have mixed up your own nightmares with your stories and films about the Holocaust. Remember that you visited the ghetto and concentration camps in Poland,' The Voice says.

'Yes, I told you that I am a storyteller.'

'But this is disgusting; you are turning everybody's stomach.'

'Why should it? What I described are bitter realities?'

'What realities? You are talking about your nightmares.'

'Oh, yes. Let me continue.'

When Ali went out of that room, a woman entered. She was wearing a veil and all of her body and face was covered. In a magical and beautiful voice, she asked me to sit next to her. I had never heard such a beautiful voice in my life. She said that she wanted to tell me a story. 'This is great,' I replied. 'I am a storyteller myself and I love stories.'

She continued: 'I know a flower which has made an ocean with her tears and is hosting millions of fish. The fish die at night with her kiss and come back to life at daybreak with another kiss from her. I kissed that flower and died and now I am waiting for the daybreak to kiss her again and come back to life. I know that soon that flower will come to me and with her magical voice say: "Hey Roxana, wake up and look at the sun on the horizon".'

I couldn't believe it. I told her: 'Your name is Roxana? It is a beautiful name.' Moments later she uncovered her face and body. She was made of flowers and leaves. From that moment my soul became prisoner of her beauties. She took me in her arms and I could feel eternal love. We swam in deep oceans and like fish enjoyed the songs of the waves. I had never felt such happiness, but suddenly Ali returned to the room and said: 'Don't smoke this opium, it makes you crazy.' I woke from my sweet dream and found myself in another nightmare. She wasn't there any more and Ali was chewing the eye of a donkey.

***

I was walking along the street of a strange town. People were speaking a foreign language. It was very different from the place where I used to live.

'You went to the west.' The Voice says.

'How? I am having a nightmare in the mountains.'

'With nightmares, you can go everywhere.'

'I had to be interviewed - why? I don't know. Here they call me an immigrant.'

'That is the polite word for fucking foreigner, ha, ha, ha.'

'You shut up.'

'Question: where have you come from?'

'Mountains, war, dictatorship and poverty.'

'A question: do you like biscuit?'

'Oh yes, I am hungry.'

'A question: so you should know Madam Biscuit?'

'No, I do not know her, although I once had a nightmare about her.'

'What about Ali's donkeys?'

'What a silly question, I did speak to Ali but I don't know his donkeys.'

'Did Ali's donkeys attack you, as well? When we X-rayed your head, we found a bruise that must have been the result of a kick from a hoof.'

'No, I don't know. What are you talking about?'

A moment later they brought Ali into the room, I couldn't believe it. He was totally changed. Now he had blonde hair and blue eyes. He started to pile stones on my shoulders. I shouted at him: 'Hey! I am not a donkey!' Others in the room started laughing and one of them said: 'Don't worry; we are going to sort you out.'

'What? What have I done?'

Someone else said: 'Oh, fucking foreigner with attitude; shut up and go away, shoo!'

****

For centuries I was walking along the streets, until one day I decided to enter a church. The church was empty and had a very clean and shiny floor. At the beginning, I was a bit nervous, but gradually the lights from the candles, the statue of a crucified man and strange quietness gave me a sense of calmness and tranquility. I sat on a chair and looked around me. Having been hungry and tired for centuries, I went to sleep. Maybe I slept for years or centuries, and when I woke up I saw the body of my best friend, the one with whom I had escaped from the army. He was covered with blood. He had been crucified and now he was dead. I looked at his body and started to cry again. Suddenly I found myself in a grave full of blood; I was drowned in blood, and I thought I was going to die. Suddenly a massive unknown force removed me from the grave and I found myself on the street again.

I kept walking, and I could see happy people, listening to music and dancing to it. For a moment I listened to the music and I felt much better. It must have been the music's magic. I said to myself: you can be happy too, like others, and decided to dance to that music, but my feet were so painful. They were bleeding. I said to myself: carry on and dance. You should feel the life and happiness through the pain and blood.

'Again you are talking about one of your novels,' says The Voice. 'In reality, you cut your wrists and this blood was coming from them.'

'Don't disturb my happiness; let me be happy for a bit. I don't want to hear your so-called "voice" again.'

****

I was a PhD student at university. One day my supervisor, who was a so-called 'professor', asked me to go to his office. First he talked a little about statistics and maths, and then he phoned someone to come to his office. A moment later, Ali entered his office with some stones in his hands. The professor asked him to put the stones on my shoulders. Surprised, I said: 'What are you doing Ali? I am not your donkey'. The professor looked at me and said: 'You know that I am working on signal processing'.

'Yes, remember, I am your student, so what?'

He said he wanted to examine the signals from my brain to my balls. I replied angrily: 'I am not your guinea pig or donkey, stop putting stones on my shoulders.' Suddenly Ali took my trousers down and first looked at my balls and than touched my buttocks, and at the same time piled more stones on my shoulders. The professor also looked at my balls and started to write down some mathematical equations.

Minutes later the professor told Ali that was enough and then said to me: 'We should go to another room; we have more tests to carry out.' He directed me to a room, where a couple of medical doctors were waiting for me with an interrogator. I sat in a chair and the interrogator said: I'll ask you questions and these doctors will examine your heart.

'Question: did you go to Madam Biscuit?'

'No, I've already told you.' Immediately after my answer, doctors examined my heart and one of them wrote something on a paper.

'Question: Are you a spy?'

'No, I am not a spy,' and again the doctors examined my heart.

'Question: Do you like the smell of flowers and ladies' perfume?'

'What a silly question, of course I like a nice smell.'

'Question: do you know Ali's donkeys?'

'I'm not going to answer these silly questions any more.' I said angrily.

The interrogator looked at the doctors' notes, and said: 'There are irregularities in your heartbeats'.

I laughed and said: 'Oh, good try! First of all there is nothing wrong with my heart and secondly your so-called "doctors" should know that people who have gone through interrogations and torture many times, and those who are facing a mountain of inquisitions, are more likely to develop heartbeat irregularities. Good try anyway.'

They wanted to continue and ask me more questions but I ran away and went to a forest.

I wanted to go back to my home, but there was a great possibility that the professor and his friends would try to examine my heart and balls again, so I went to a forest. Now it was night and I lay down close to a tree. It was windy. For a moment I thought I am in that special place on the mountain again, but I knew it was impossible. I was in western society. Hours later, I went to sleep and had a little nap. When I woke up, I was thirsty and there was no water around. As I was lying next to the tree, I remembered a fictional monster called "Al". When I was a child my parents used to mention the name of that monster to deter and prevent me from doing anything wrong. They used to say if you're naughty "Al" will take you away. "Al" was supposed to be a woman with the big breasts. Her breasts are so big she puts each one of them over her shoulder in order to carry them. I was a bit afraid when I remembered her, but suddenly a massive lady's breast came down from the top of the tree and stood in front of my eyes, then a beautiful voice said: 'Drink, drink, I know you are very thirsty.' I couldn't resist and started to suck the breast and drank lots of milk. When I finished drinking, she came down from the tree, totally naked. She put her massive breasts on her shoulders, kissed me and was gone. When she was going I shouted: 'I am sorry, I always thought you were a monster, I was wrong, you saved my life.' She just smiled at me and disappeared. I have never seen her again.

I spent weeks, months, and years in that forest.

One day I saw Ali there and asked him: 'What are you doing here?' He said: 'Who is Ali? Here my name is Mr Smith.' I said: 'Ali or Mr Smith, you should leave my ass alone. I am not one of your donkeys.' Suddenly he started to cry blood and said: 'Even you believe this gossip. I have never done any bad things to my donkeys. I have loved them. They just ridicule me because I am mad.' I thought yes, he is right. I shouldn't fall for this rubbish. I went closer to him and said: 'I am sorry, I never believed that nonsense, please forgive me'. Moments later, strangely he changed. He changed into a beautiful woman. With great surprise, I asked him: 'What has happened? You look like a beautiful lady now. Look you have got great breasts.' I thought it was the magic of "Al".

Ali with a big smile on his or her lips said: 'Now I am Ms Smith, look how beautiful I am in these black clothes'. I looked at her beauty and told her that she was very beautiful, and I asked her if I could have a kiss. She came closer to me, and suddenly slapped my face, and with great anger said: 'I have always known that you wanted to fuck my donkeys.'

****

Part (3)
Hopeless human with terrifying nightmares tends towards
safe haven/ fantasises
Introduction to Mr H and films
(... and human created his/her God...)

'Good news! I have very good news for you.' The Voice said.

'Oh, not you again, what do you want from me?'

'You have been selected to go to the Oscars.'

'You must be joking. Why me?'

'Everybody knows how much you like films. You have been chosen for your hard work and your dedication to writing beautiful stories for films.'

'Am I not supposed to be in a nightmare?'

'You will find out.'

I looked at myself in the mirror. Oh God; my clothes were disastrous for any kind of ceremony. How could I go there in these clothes? I've even forgotten how to wear a tie. Suddenly I was in a Superman costume, and started to fly to Hollywood. I got there in a very short time and found myself in my previous clothes, facing the door of an office. I entered the office and saw a very famous actor sitting behind a desk. He looked at me and said: 'Oh, you, I am glad that you are here. Do you know that the ceremony will start tomorrow?' I said I did, and with great excitement told him, 'I can't believe that you wanted me to be here. I love your acting, especially that film about people with the mental illnesses. With that film, you brought massive enlightenment and knowledge to many people, and I personally think you were brilliant in that film. Winning the Oscar was well deserved.'

He smiled and said: 'That was a very good film and I was so lucky to be part of it. Anyway let's talk about the job.'

'Job? What job? Surely you don't want me to give a speech? I am so nervous, this is my first time.'

He looked at me, surprised, and said: 'Who said that you were going to be part of the ceremony?'

'The Voice told me.'

He shook his head and said: 'Somebody told me before that you are a little bit retarded. Listen, we don't have much time. Tomorrow's ceremony is going ahead and I have a million things to do.'

'What do you want me to do?'

He said: 'Wait a minute, I will tell you soon,' and then made a phone call. A moment later two big security guards with two very big boxes came into the room. He stood up and said to me: 'Go and look inside the boxes.' I looked. They were full of Oscar trophies for the winners of different categories. Seconds later he asked the security guards to put these boxes on my shoulders. I couldn't believe it. They also thought that I was a donkey. I said to him angrily: 'I am not a donkey, what are you doing?'

For seconds he looked at me with a very serious face, and suddenly started to dance. Every time that he shook his butt or belly, I could hear a sound similar to church bells. I already knew that some of these actors are a bit mad and unusual, but that dance and those noises were so strange. Sometime later he stopped and stared at me. I didn't know what I should say or do; I was very confused.

Eventually I thought of something and told him: 'Ha, you used the noise of church bells to remind me of a film about church, its name was *The De Vinci Code*. I saw that film, but I swear, I haven't been involved in any conspiracy, and I have never gone to Madam Biscuit's place, and I haven't followed Ali's donkeys, and I am not a dangerous criminal. I am just a writer and I think I am good at writing subjects, which are good for films.'

He shook his head and started to dance again. This time he was lap dancing. He came closer to me and suddenly like a stripper, ripped apart his trousers, and stood in front of me. I couldn't believe it, his balls were so big. He shook his butt and belly and I could see clearly that the church-bell noise came from the impact of his balls together. He covered himself with a cloth, and said: 'You think getting to the position I am now, is easy? Did you see my balls? I worked hard to achieve this, now my balls are bigger than my head, because I have worked very hard.'

I said to him: 'I believe you. I know hard work is essential, but it's not all about hard work. I think all of us are agreed that Ali's donkeys work harder than anybody; I think it is a matter of providing opportunities too. So you are lucky that you were given opportunities.'

He asked me to go with him to the corner of the room, and then opened a carton and said: 'Look at them.' It was a big picture of some very famous actresses, and all of them in that picture had very big breasts. They put their breasts on their shoulders. Immediately I remembered The "Al", my fictional childhood character. He took me to another corner of the room, and revealed a second picture. It was a picture of some famous actors. All of them had massive balls. Finally he showed me a picture of a black man; only his face was clear in the picture and the rest of his body was covered and censored. He said: 'For security reasons, we cannot show all of his body, but if I and my fellow actors have balls this size, imagine how big his balls are! Now don't waste our time and go.' Before I left his office, he told one of the security guards: 'Examine his balls while he is carrying these boxes, and report back to me.' And then told me: 'Send a copy of your life story to me.'

'My life story? Oh not again. Why? There is nothing interesting in my autobiography, except war, blood and suffering.'

'You never know: we may make a film based on your life,' he said.

Before I flew back, I saw a famous actor sitting on his car and eating Biscuits!

****

Spring is coming. I can smell the beauty of flowers. Flowers are carrying the blood of lovers. Spring is coming and spreading a special message, the message is: 'love and love and love,' we should love each other, and we should love nature and all the creatures that exist in it. Spring is the season of lovers. It must be in spring that the amorous poet wrote his poem of love:

A slaughterer was crying
He has lost his heart to a little canary. (5)

Spring is coming and brings our New Year with her. The first day of spring is our New Year. I have always liked New Year. I remember the excitement of having new shoes or clothes. I remember my father used to keep new money notes inside the Koran and at New Year give them to me, and my brothers and sister. I remember an old lady; I learned from her how to press flowers in my notebooks; they would smell nice even when they dried. I never saw my grandmother because she was dead before I was born. The old lady was the second wife of my grandfather and she was very good to me because of my disability. She was always giving special love and attention to me; love and attention that I am still craving and missing.

'Your dreams are too sweet, don't forget that you are in your nightmare.'

'Oh, it's you, the bloody Voice again.'

New Year is coming and I should prepare myself for celebration. No matter how hard life is, I am going to enjoy the New Year. I should have asked that actor in Hollywood to come here as my guest. I could show him real hospitality. What was his name? I don't remember, so I'll call him Mr H.

'Hello, are you there?'

'Is that you, bloody Voice again?'

'Voice? No, I am Mr H, you asked me to join you for New Year.'

'Oh, I was just thinking about you, please come in. Would you like anything to eat or drink?'

'No, thanks, you wanted to show me your exciting New Year traditions. I might get some ideas for a film.'

'I am so glad that you are here, this is the magic of spring and our New Year; you came here at this time of the year, and you're talking about ideas for films. You know how much I like films. Your arrival at this time of the year is proof of the spirit of spring and our New Year. Come here, I want to show you something special. Yesterday I went to the market and bought two little red fishes. This is our tradition, to gather beautiful little fish, some special food, mirrors, flowers and green grass into our homes, to welcome the arrival of New Year. Come and look at my beautiful fish.'

Mr H looked at the fish, and suddenly with great fear in his face and a shaky voice said: 'These are not fish; there are two eyes in the water.' I looked at them, and realised that, yes, there were two eyes in the water. They must belong to Jack. Jack was a young male character in one of my stories; my stories also came to be with me in the New Year. My stories are always with me, they never leave me. I said to Mr H: 'Don't worry, these have come from one of my stories, I called that story *Their Eyes* and it is a great story, and perfect for a film.' When I said that, the flower next to the mirror started to cry, and for a second I saw the face of Mr H in the mirror. He was crying too, crying blood. Moments later he wiped the blood off his face and with a very sad voice said: 'I don't want to be in your films.'

'You mean my nightmares?'

'Films, nightmares or your madness, I don't want to be here.'

'Don't worry, nobody can harm you, you must be suffering from culture shock, I know how hard it is; when I escaped and became a refugee in the west, I suffered severe culture shock. I should have told you that you may suffer from it as well.'

'This is not culture shock. I am already familiar with lots of different cultures. It is about you and your nightmares.'

'Okay, let's get out of this place. I am sorry that I upset you.'

'Upset? You are making me mad, like yourself.'

'Sorry, let me take you out and show you my home-town and places that I used to play when I was a child. First I'll show you a football pitch, but don't be surprised; it is very different from football pitches in your country. It is a very dirty and dusty piece of land, but I'll never forget the excitement of playing football there. Although I was disabled and had problems with my legs, I still could enjoy the game. Now let's go out.'

We went out and walked towards the football pitch. There were some people gathering and we could hear the groans of a man. When we got closer, we saw a man had been tied to a table and someone was lashing him. I asked an old man in the crowd: 'What has he done?' The old man who was crying said: 'He spoke the forbidden word loudly.'

'What is the forbidden word?'

'Love: love, my son. The forbidden word is love. We are not allowed to mention this word, it is forbidden.'

Mr H, with a fearful face said: 'Let's get away from here. Let me get out of your nightmares; I don't want to be here.'

'Sorry Mr H, this is not the message of spring or New Year. We had better go somewhere else,' and we both ran away.

Sometime later I told him: 'Come this way, I want to show you one of my best friends. Don't worry, she is not a human and she doesn't carry any hatred within herself. When I was scared or sad, she used to be my refuge. She is a tree, and I am going to introduce you to her.'

'Oh, you have gone to another one of your stories, haven't you?' The Voice said.

'Yes, my dear Voice, why not? My stories are always with me.'

Mr H looked at me and said: 'Who are you talking to?'

'The Voice. Don't worry I am the only one that can see or hear it. Come on, we are close to my friend, the tree. Here she is, I used to see her every day on my way to school.' We got close to the tree, but my tree wasn't alone; a woman was hanging from one of her branches and they were both dancing splendidly in the wind; the dance was the dance of death, and the hanged woman was the woman of my dreams. I have loved her all my life without knowing her; I don't even know what her name is. I named her Roxana, and now Roxana the Goddess of Beauty was doing her last dance. I hadn't noticed that I was crying blood, until Mr H asked: 'Who is she and why are you crying blood?'

'She is eternal love, soul of spring; look at her eyes; no colour and no beauty match her eyes. Look at them, look how the tree and the

Goddess of Beauty are dancing amorously. Come closer Mr H, come dance with me, we should join them.'

'But I don't know the dance of death.'

'I'll show you, it is similar to a waltz.' We both started to dance a slow waltz, and at the same time were crying blood.

Minutes later, Mr H said again: 'I don't want to be in your films. Let me go.'

'Yes, let's go from here. We're both trapped in this land of death, run, run,' and we both ran. While we were running, I told him that I remembered one particular film: it was about a young disabled boy, and the girl he was in love with asked him to run, because she didn't want him to be harmed by the bad boys. I know how hard it is to be bullied. I also was bullied at school because I was disabled. It happened in real life, not in my nightmares. He suddenly stopped and said: 'Don't mix films with your nightmares; I don't want to be part of it. Now tell me which way we should go? I have to go back to my country.'

We walked for hours, and came to a hill where again we saw a group of people gathering. Mr H said: 'We shouldn't get close to them, I am sure something horrible is going on there too.' I said: 'We need to ask someone which way to go,' and than we went close to the crowd, and saw an unbelievable and shocking scene; a woman was buried up to her chest in the ground and some people were throwing stones at her. With great fear and disgust, I asked a man: 'Why do they do this? What has she done to be killed in this horrific way?'

'She did a forbidden act; the act of love. Love is forbidden; long live barbarism.'

I looked at the terrified face of Mr H and said: 'This is not the message of spring.' Mr H was in a state of shock.

I shouted at him: 'Run, run, run away from this madness,' and when he was running, he shouted: 'I don't want to be in your nightmares, no, I don't, leave me alone.' He did continue to run for many years.

****

I was in the battlefield in a desert. Dead bodies were scattered everywhere. I was with a group of young boys; they were child soldiers. We were under heavy bombardment by enemy jet fighters and artillery units. It was a real hell. Bombs, bolts and shells were harvesting young lives. I wished I could protect them, but the scythe of death was so strong and brutal. Some time later, I found myself alone in that desert; it was just me and the dead bodies. The sun was extremely hot and brutal; perhaps Sun had learned brutality from humanity. The sunlight exposed the bodies and burnt desert very clearly, as if it wanted to remind me every moment of humanity's contemptuousness. The Earth was also crying; so many young blossoms of life were faded. I was left alone with the sorrowing flowers, I couldn't even cry any more, alone; alone; alone with profound bewilderment; the splendour of life left me and I learned the depth of death; alone, bewildered and tired.

In that vast desert there was only one tree, on the line of the horizon. Was it a tree or a mirage? I needed to escape from this burning sun. I had to find some shadow, why was night not coming? At least the darkness could cover and hide these dead bodies from my eyes. I had to go to that tree. When I got close to the tree, I saw Mr H looking at the woman who was hanged from the branch. I looked at Mr H's puzzled face and asked: 'What are you doing here?' But he didn't notice me, he was miles away, he looked mystified. I got closer to him, and put my hand on his shoulder and said: 'Mr H, are you all right?' He looked at me with frozen eyes, and said: 'Look at her. They hanged the woman of my dreams. Look at her, they killed the Goddess of Beauty.' and he started to cry bitterly.

For a moment I looked at the hanged woman, and then told Mr H: 'She is not the woman of your dreams, she is the woman of my dreams. Look at her carefully. You don't even know her name. I also don't know her name, I just call her Roxana. This is Roxana; there was an ocean between us. That ocean separated me from her for centuries.

Sun had promised me
She would dry an ocean
The ocean between me and her
I used to see her on the horizon
Horizon; place, where the ocean joins the sky
Sun delivered her promise
The ocean dried up
And I, with the ocean of love in my heart
Walked for years towards the horizon
Now, I have reached the horizon
Reached the sky
Reached her seat of martyrdom
Horizon; a place, where blood joins the vast emptiness,
A place, where pain reaches the depth of the soul
A place, for the dance of death
Endless line of mystery

Horizon; our trysting place (6)

'I was waiting all this time for the heat of the sun to evaporate the water, so I could walk to her. What do you think Mr H; do you think this hot sun has dried the ocean?'

He looked at me angrily and said: 'I told you before; I don't want to be in your films or nightmares, what do you want from me?'

'Nothing, I didn't ask you to be here, you came here by yourself. Look, you're even wearing military uniform: maybe when you were playing in your war movie you got lost and ended up here.'

'No, it's you! I'm lost in your terrifying nightmares. Show me the way out. I don't want to be here.'

'Okay, come with me, we have to walk for a long time.'

It took us years to pass through that desert which was covered in dead bodies; it had to be a dried-up ocean. We walked for years in strange silence, I was thinking all these years how can I start to talk to Mr H again, until I remembered a poem, which I recited to him:

Special mementos of life
Always would be presented in silence
Friendship and love
Happiness and pain
Birth and death
Flower and rising of the sun
And silence; in lieu of profound space of sagacity (wisdom) (7)

I told him that poem had been one source of my inspiration for writing a story. I called that story *The Last Scene*, and again I thought it would be a very good subject for a film, but it was very political, and I didn't think it would be made by Hollywood. He didn't want to talk about films so we continued walking for several more years.

One thing that we didn't know was that we were walking through a time tunnel backwards. Finally we found ourselves in a ghetto in Poland. Mr H, with great surprise on his face, looked at me and said: 'Where are we?' For a moment I looked around, and than told him: 'Oh, I know this place, I have been here before. We are in a ghetto in Poland.' Mr H angrily replied: 'Why did you take me here?'

'I didn't want to, but it seems we have walked back through time and history. Look at these people, they are all starving. I did some research for one of my stories, and I have read about the situation here; it must be a hell on earth.'

'How many times have I to tell you that I don't want to be in your stories, nightmares or films. I don't belong here.'

'Nor do I, we are here now and we have to fight for our survival. Both of us are physically fit and we can get a job here.'

Very soon we found a job, which was to remove the starved dead bodies to the graveyard and bury them. Every day we collected dead bodies and put them in our wagon and took them to the graveyard.

'So, again, you are in your story'.

'Oh Voice again, Yes I am.'

'Who are you talking to? Are you going mad?' Mr H said.

'Don't worry Mr H, I was talking to the Voice. If you want to survive, we have to work very hard.'

In the first several hours of our work, we had collected five or six dead bodies and taken them to the graveyard. Mr H was still in a state of shock and couldn't believe what was going on. The graveyard was very peaceful; at least death brought rest for these people. Mr H was scared and came close to me and said: 'I am terrified; we have to escape from here, we don't belong here.'

'Where we can go? We have no place to go; with this job at least we can find some food and clothes to protect ourselves from cold and starvation. I know for sure how this thing is going to end.'

'How do you know?'

'I told you that I did some research for my story; I have read about the ghettos and concentration camps.'

One day there was a massive invasion of the ghetto and a round-up of Jews carried out by the SS and German soldiers. They took me and Mr H and large numbers of men, women and children and put us on a train. Each wagon of the train was massively overcrowded. We hardly got any rest. They didn't tell us where we were going, but I knew this was a death train and we were going to the death camps. It was a very difficult journey, especially when we saw the suffering of these people and their children. It was a nightmare trip, but I knew that the real nightmare hadn't started yet and was ahead of us.

I told Mr H that we were going to Auschwitz; we must be careful when we got there. We should pretend that we were healthy and strong; otherwise they would take us to the gas chamber and kill us.

We were lucky; we had been selected to go to the Auschwitz concentration camp. In front of the camp there was written this sentence: *Arbeit macht frei*, work gives freedom, I told Mr H that we must be very strong and positive; the average life expectancy for prisoners was just a few months. They put a special tattoo on our left arms and immediately we had to start our slavery. I said to Mr H:

'Don't worry; I know for sure that we will both survive.' Mr H with great fear in his face said: 'How do you know that we are going to survive?'

'Because we are from the future. I promise you we will both survive and you will become a great actor, trust me, I know this for sure.'

Every day living and surviving there was a miracle. One day for no apparent reason, Mr H and I were sent to punishment cells. They were dark and very small and we had to stand for hours. Several days later, they took us out of our cells for execution. There was a special place for execution. It was a yard surrounded by some buildings. There was a wall that was partly covered by cement and victims had to stand in front of that wall to be shot. When I saw Mr H's face in the daylight, I realised that he had given in to death. I looked at his fearful and puzzled face and said: 'Do you know what? You remind me of one of your characters in your famous film. He was also weak as he approached death. But don't worry; as I said before, we both will survive. We went closer to the wall and I asked him quietly to put his forehead on the cement of the wall. We both put our foreheads on the cold cement of the wall; it was a very difficult time, we were both expecting to be shot at any moment. While we stood there, I whispered to him: 'This cold cement also reminds me of a prison cell in Iraq. I was a prisoner there, and in order to hear other prisoners next to my cell, I had to put my head and face to the cold wall of my cell. I could hear their moaning and pain, when they were tortured as they are here. I was expecting to be the next victim. Waiting for death and to be tortured is so difficult.'

We stayed there for days, weeks and months; the executioners were so busy killing others that they forgot about us. I knew a miracle was going to happen, and we would survive.

*****

Now we were both journalists, and had a chance to enter Buchenwald concentration camp shortly after its liberation. It was spring 1945. We witnessed some shocking scenes, including a large number of starved dead bodies, even shrunken heads and tattooed skin used for lampshades. They were unbelievable scenes. I looked at the sad face of Mr H and said: 'You look very sick, maybe depression is taking hold of your mind.'

He looked at me and shook his head and said: 'Look, we are not in a film. These things that we are witnessing have happened in reality.' And then he asked: 'Aren't we in spring?'

'Yes, it is spring of 1945.'

'What has happened to the spirit of spring? The soul of spring that you were talking about - wasn't spring suppose to bring about love?' And moments later he started to cry and said: 'Where was God all of this time?' He continued and said: 'Please take me out of your nightmares, I can't continue. I am losing my faith in God, humanity and spring. I don't know what to do without them. I am scared; show me the way out of here.'

In the absence of humanity on earth
Satan celebrates
A Celebration of blood and fire
Burning, men, women and children
With yellow stars on their chests
Stripped of the spirit of spring
 Victims of a loveless earth
  And guests of Satan's celebration
That's what happens when humanity leaves the earth (8)

****

Darkness; I never knew that one day I would prefer darkness to light. Now I am in absolute darkness. I can't see anything, but I prefer this darkness; I am blindfolded and I can't see the ugly faces of torturers. I can't see their victims with their blood and bruises. I wish there was a way of not hearing them as well. They push me around and direct me to go somewhere; I know that they are taking me to the torture chamber.

'Oh, again you have gone to one of your stories.'

'Yes, Voice, do you have a problem with that?'

'No, absolutely not.'

'So, shut up and leave me alone.'

Now I can hear the moaning voice of someone under torture, I must be close to the torture chamber.

An interrogator asked me to sit down close to a wall and be silent. I asked him: 'How long do I have to wait here?' In response, he punched and kicked me and said: 'I told you to be silent; you are going to wait here as long as we like, so sit down and shut up.'

I sat there silently and he left. After a while, I found some strength and courage to move a little bit of my blindfold, so I could see what was going on around me. I was sitting in a room half-full of blindfolded prisoners. Some of them were lying down, covered in their own blood. They were the ones who had already been tortured. Hearing the voices of moaning prisoners was terrifying and extremely sad. I needed to talk to someone in order to distract myself from these frightening voices. I looked at the prisoner next to me and asked him: 'Are you okay?' When he turned his head towards me, I couldn't believe that it was Mr H, who was blindfolded and was sitting next to me. He was very scared to say anything. With great surprise and sadness I said: 'Hey, Mr H it is me, remember me? I took you into my stories, films and my nightmares. Don't worry, you are going to be all right, they are going to release you and you can go back to America.' Mr H said in a frightened voice: 'You have no right to take me into your bloody nightmares. This time I am going to die; they have tortured me, they want me to tell everybody that I am a spy. I am not a spy, I haven't done anything against people of this country, but they want to use me as propaganda for their policies. I have been kept close to this torture chamber for hours and I can't stay in this situation any longer. This is the worst type of torture; these moaning voices are killing me.'

Suddenly two interrogators had started to punch and kick us because we didn't notice that they were coming over to us and we were not supposed to talk to each other. Several hours later they took us both to the torture chamber. They tied me to the torture bed first, and started to lash my feet. At the beginning I wanted to control myself and not moan or shout loudly because I didn't want to make Mr H any more scared, but it was impossible. After a couple of lashes I started to moan and shout loudly. Some time later somebody forced a dirty and bloody piece of cloth into my mouth to silence me. Pain combined with the sense of suffocation was so great that I thought I was going to die very soon. I was about to join the eternal darkness: death. I had never known that one day I would prefer eternal darkness to life. I had never known that one day darkness would be a way to freedom; freedom from pain and torture.

I woke up when somebody poured some cold water on my face. I must have been unconscious. I came painfully back to life again. Now I didn't have any blindfold on my eyes and I saw Mr H standing in the corner of the room, crying. Moments later he said in a scared and shaky voice: 'Okay, you are telling me that I am a spy. Okay, I am a spy; I admit that I am a spy, what else do you want from me?'

One of the interrogators looked at me and said: 'Did you hear that? He admitted that he is a spy. Now you can see that we are targeted by the Americans. We have to defend our country; people like you are opposed to our government, helping our enemies.'

They put Mr H and me into a cell. We talked for hours, days and months. I could feel that for him the situation was much harder than for anybody else. He wasn't used to such a brutal and harsh environment.

One day, when we had both put our foreheads to the cold cement wall of our cell to hear the other prisoners outside, he asked me why I was arrested.

I said: 'I was looking for Roxana, the Goddess of Beauty, but they arrested me. Looking for beauties is a crime here.' He was silent for a moment and than said: 'Did you say Roxana?'

'Yes, Roxana - well, *I* have named her Roxana.'

He looked at me and in a very sad voice said: 'Several months ago, the prison authorities took all the prisoners to the yard to witness the hanging of Roxana. She was the Goddess of Beauty, and she was and still is the woman of my dreams. Before her death she told me that she had never believed that I was a spy, that she and all other prisoners knew that I was an innocent man, just like the rest of us. Since then, she has become the woman of my dreams.' Mr H continued to cry bitterly and said: 'She even smiled at me when she was hanging; she died with a smile on her lips. The last thing that I learned from her was the dance of death. She was dancing with the tree splendidly; the dance of death.'

*****

Part (4)
Human with Endless
Nightmares Seeks Cure

Oh, my god, I had never been as relaxed and comfortable as this. It was as if I was awake and tortured for many years and now suddenly I found myself in absolute calm and tranquility. Maybe I was dead and heaven existed after all. I didn't want to open my eyes and find myself tied to a torture bed again. Some delicate hands were massaging my feet and hands and someone was holding my head. These hands must have belonged to women, who were so comforting and tender.

After many years in harsh situations, this was the first time I had felt good. I only felt a bit thirsty.

Moments later, one of the hands that were holding my head opened my mouth and poured some delicious liquid into it. I didn't know what it was, but it tasted amazing. After that the same hand wiped my mouth with something very soft and delicate, something like a woman's breast. I couldn't resist any more and opened my eyes. It was unbelievable; I was in a clean and comfortable bed and surrounded by beautiful naked women. One of them was wiping my mouth and lips with her breast and others were massaging my feet and hands. Until then, I thought there was only one "Al", but now I was with five of them and surprisingly each one of them was from a different part of the world; Africa, Europe, Asia…and so on.

'Ha, ha, ha, from bloody nightmares to fucking fantasy.'

'Damn Voice! Is that you again? As far as I remember you started as a teacher or adviser to me but over time you've become increasingly dirtier and nastier.'

'Don't worry; this is part of your cure.'

'Oh, are you sure? Is it not because you didn't get what you wanted?'

'I told you it is for your own good.'

'My own good? I think you need a psychiatrist yourself! Go away and leave me alone.'

Suddenly I noticed that all these women were looking at me in surprise. Then one of them with a very calm and warm voice said: 'You must have been in a nightmare, don't worry, you are safe here'. All of them started to massage me again.

Minutes later Mr H entered our room. He was naked and had just covered his lower body with a towel. He smiled at me and came closer and said: 'How are you? You are in the best hands.' I looked at him and suddenly shouted at him: 'You bastard, you set me up with these women! I told you before that I have never been in Madam Biscuit's places, my principles don't allow me to be in this situation.' Mr H in great surprise said: 'Who do you think you are? A president! That is why you are always afraid of scandalous news, Ha?'

'You don't have to be a president to be set up or become a victim of a smear campaign; it can happen at any level and to anybody.'

'Not to you, I just wanted to help you. From the first time that I met you, I've noticed you're very suspicious of everything.'

'Yes, that is part of my mental illness.'

'Don't worry, nobody wants to set you up, just relax and enjoy your treatments.'

'Treatments? Where am I?'

'Sex clinic. And these ladies are sex experts.'

'I knew that you were a womaniser, I remember one of your films: in that film you were playing a womaniser, but to be honest it wasn't a great film - actually far from it. I hope my criticism doesn't make you angry.'

'No, I am an actor, and many times have been criticised. This is part of our job, and I know perfectly well myself that I appeared in some movies that weren't good. For your information, I must say that I have a girlfriend, and I'm not looking for anybody else. Now look at these ladies, this is equal opportunities in practice: each one of them is from a different continent.'

'So what are you doing here?'

'To get some treatment. After being in your terrifying nightmares, films and stories, I desperately need some treatments. Now you'd better relax.'

'I am glad you mentioned this is a sex clinic because I have an idea for a film.'

He smiled and said: 'Very good, when you manage to write it, send a copy to me.' Then he looked at the women and said: 'Okay dear ladies, you'd better start. Hopefully you will manage to dewankcutise him, I know he was wankcuted badly,' and then went out of our room.

The process of DEWANKCUTION is very explicit for this story. Maybe I should think of writing a film script...

*****

I was in the psychiatric hospital; a place full of people carrying thousands of strange and scary thoughts. A world of wonder; a world with its own twisted logic, a world of silence, a world of damaged souls, a world of broken images, a place to fall into oblivion, an alternative to chains and cells. This is to think and recuperate, a place where hope is hidden behind the horizon, but still not forgotten. A place to rest, a place to stop the clocks and free damaged souls from the relentlessness of depression, anxiety and pain. It's a place to learn about crushed souls, a place for mending fragile human dignity and a place to die.

Mr H was also there, but he was refusing to talk to anyone. He was spending hours looking at an unknown horizon. Maybe he was acting - acting upon the poem that once I read to him - and the silence was in lieu of the profound space of sagacity. Maybe he was acting like that big Indian man in the film *One Flew Over the Cuckoo's Nest*. Maybe he was exploring the situation for a future role.

On one lonely grey day of autumn, he left the hospital. I was happy that he had family and loved-ones who could look after him. That day, I noticed that his hair had turned grey. Grey was the dominant colour of the hospital.

> **My friend's hair wasn't black any more**
> **His hair, like the dust that covers the bottle of wine, was grey**
> **I have never liked the grey**
> **Grey reminds me of exile**
> **Grey is like a lonely day in autumn**
> **Grey represents the journey between dream and logic, heat and cold, life and death**
> **Grey is like my fate, to be far away and a stranger**
> **Grey is like the dirty minds of monsters and witches, ridiculing life and hope**
> **I wish at least my friend's hair was white**
> **The same white as when a wave kisses a beach**
> **No, I have never liked the grey**
> ****
> **On one stormy night when we were lost in our past memories, a light gave us this message: wait, wait**
> **Wait for white**
> **The same white that is like the heart of an angel**
> **Wait, wait**
> **Wait for white lilies on your grave**
> ****
> **Grey is like my fate, to be far away and a stranger**
> **No, I have never liked grey**

59

Maybe I should talk more about red

Yes red, the impact of the lash on raw skin, or blue like an empty sky

An empty sky that impatiently waits to be looked at by her beautiful eyes

But grey reminds me that I have been away from her

Grey reminds me of the ashes of fires from bombs and bullets

I wish the world was more colourful

Colourful like our friendship, colourful like love

Grey is hopelessness

Grey is the death of love

In prison I never got used to the grey walls of my cell

I have never forgotten the grey voices of prisoners and their pain

No, I have never liked grey

*****

On one moonlit night

Moonlight had drawn a shiny silver road on the surface of an ocean

The silver road was going to the end of the ocean, to the horizon

It was on that road and that horizon that I saw her

An angel with a basket of flowers

I knew that kissing an angle on the horizon was a perilous thrill, but temptation was so great, like one moonstruck

I began to walk on the silver road towards the angel on the horizon

I never got to the horizon; I went to the bottom of the ocean

The bottom of the ocean wasn't shiny silver any more, it was grey

I remembered a great poet: Federico Garcia Lorca

I remembered his death, execution on a grey day

I remembered his song about the moon: go moon, go, go moon…

Yes it was a night of madness

In the mad house I had to be injected with grey medicine

Living with the grey mad, and watching the grey moonlight at nights

No, I have never liked grey   (9)

*****

I was looking from the window of the psychiatric unit to the street; people were going through their ordinary day to day lives. Ordinary? What does that mean? Does it mean, getting married, having kids, going to work daily, growing old and finally dying? That's so boring,

60

even more boring than being here. What transforms the ordinary to the extraordinary? Love? Perhaps love is the answer, but here I can't think of love. If there were enough love in our world I and others wouldn't end up here.

One of the nurses who knew Mr H was my friend came to me and said: 'You must be feeling lonely now, especially after Mr H leaving.' I said: 'Don't worry about me, I am very familiar with loneliness, and I am not the only person in this world that is alone.' She said: 'I want to introduce you to another patient; he is from your country too. His name is Mohammad; he is a very funny and good man.

'Look he is sitting in that corner.' I looked at him. I had already seen him in the ward but I didn't want to talk to him. He was a big fat man, with a shaved head, and his face was covered with a long beard. He reminded me of some religious fanatics, who were supporting the Iranian regime. When the nurse said that he was from Iran, I thought, oh, so even here these killers are watching me; he must be working for the Iranian government. I remembered our situation in that special place in the mountains that was full of spies. I said to the nurse: 'I don't want to know him.'

Several weeks later, one day he came to me and said in Farsi: 'I saw you had a visitor, and you were speaking Farsi, I am from Iran too.' I asked him: 'Why are you here?' He said: 'I was a scientist but my wife made a bet on my brain and lost it, so I became stupid. Even all the doctors and nurses are betting on my brain. The other day a doctor and a nurse took me to a room and then the nurse started to massage the doctor's dick and wank him, and when the doctor came, they took the doctor's juice and injected it into my head. It was very painful. Here everybody is a cannibal, every day they knife me and take part of my body to eat. Be careful, they may bet on your brain too. The devils are everywhere, they use black magic. The other day I went out to sleep with a prostitute, but she was a devil. She put all my head and body into her posy. It was very scary. Be careful here, everybody is a dragon, even you. Can I have a fag?' It was the beginning of our friendship and we are still friends.

It was in that hospital that I experienced love again. I fell in love with a girl, who was a patient in another ward of the same hospital. Love could find its way even there. I started to love her through my madness and lost her through my stupidity.

*****

61

Years after I had been discharged from the psychiatric hospital, I went to see a professor of psychology to ask his opinion about my mental state. When I entered his office, he was sitting behind his desk and several other people were also sitting around his desk. The professor with a big smile came close to me and shook my hand and asked me to sit on a chair. Moments later he said: 'I am very glad that you are here; you wanted to know what was or is wrong with you, and how we managed to make you feel better, ha?'

'Yes, of course.'

'Well, I have to start with some definitions; as you experienced it, paranoia is a mental illness which causes delusions of grandeur or persecution in the form of intense fear or suspicion.'

'Yes of course, I have experienced that in practice, and I know exactly what you are talking about.'

'Excellent, we also know, schizophrenia is a very frightening, very debilitating illness. Sufferers have wild association of thought that can often be of a paranoid or persecutory nature. In order to continue further, I would like to emphasise several key words in that definition - pay particular attention to these words. Sufferers have wild association of thoughts. This is crucial to remember: according to one of our distinguished psychologists and several researchers, in this capacity they - sufferers of schizophrenia - have to put ideas and images together in unusual ways. This is also characteristic of many artists. If schizophrenics can find a way to translate their thoughts into art, then the results can be extremely powerful and in some cases they can also be extremely harrowing. The link between madness and artistic creativity has long been suspected. Rates of mental illness are hugely elevated in the families of poets, writers and artists, suggesting that the same genes, temperaments and imaginative capacities lie behind both insanity and creative ability. So we decided to find a way to communicate with you and go through your mind, in order to make you feel better.'

'How? I don't think that you have started from the very beginning.'

'Yes of course, I must tell you that this was an expensive and delicate operation. First we had to know you better, so we started to collect information about you from various sources, and then we had to observe you closely for a long time. Thanks to new technology these days we can do that easily.'

'In other words, put me under surveillance.'

'Don't take it that way; it is for your own good.'

'Oh really!'

'As I said, in order to find out your thoughts and their associations, the key thing to do was to identify your passions. It was obvious from the beginning that you like films and writing.'

'So you needed to boost my ego, ha?'

'Next step was to create associations, which are controllable by us. This was a delicate operation too; we needed precise timing and actions. So, based on our knowledge about you - your writing, your talking, your history...etc - we managed to create those associations.'

'What are these associations?'

'Various things. It can be an object; as you know an object in schizophrenia goes abstract; it can be a colour, a human being, a voice...etc. By observing you, it was easy to find out where you were going, what you were watching, what you were eating...etc'

'How did creating these so-called "associations" help me or you?'

'Aha, by managing to create these associations, we can control and manipulate the thoughts, so we can remove the obstacles and problems from the mind of a schizophrenic and give them more mental strength. As I said before, it is a very delicate operation; it is a powerful tool for education and has several applications; psychology, art, entertainment and police work. Of course there are issues regarding privacy and civil rights, but don't worry, you are in safe hands.'

'I should read the book *1984* one more time; isn't it characteristic of minds of some or many sufferers that they believe their thoughts are controlled by mysterious agencies?'

'Yes, it is true.'

'But in reality you are doing it to me.'

'As I said, in this way we managed to make you feel much better.'

'I don't think you'd be able to draw conclusions from my fictional stories and get the true results. I noticed on many occasions that you got it totally wrong. Actually you and your associates act upon your guesses and suspicions, which have nothing to do with my realities, either past or present. I just see them as rubbish accusations; to be honest, I react to your suspicions and paranoia. When you create a fake environment you get fake results. In fact you create your own fictions, and every time that I see the actions of one of your agents or my associate, I have to go through hell to find out what your plan is, or what new accusation you're levelling at me. Of course you are telling me that bombarding me with your dirty accusations is good for my mental state. But how?'

'You know that fear of accusations is part of the illness.'

'I knew you were going to say that, but I have learned an important fact.'

'What?'

'The fact that environment plays a more important role in relation to the individual. In my case it may be true that I inherited genes that rendered me vulnerable to mental illnesses, but it is the *environment* that triggers these illnesses. If I became ill in my past brutal environments, I have regained health (almost) here, in my new environment. So in fact, the practical act of changing my surroundings and environment helped me to change my perceptions and deal with my illness. Actually I should discuss this with Mr H.'

'Who is Mr H?'

'My associate - oh now you know him. He is also going to play a manipulative role.'

'What do you want to discuss with him?'

'Mr H is an actor and in one of his films he played a character who had to be in psychiatric detention. I am sure, through his research for that film, he must have noticed how much ignorance and prejudice surrounded that illness. So in the film he was trying to change people's perceptions in that particular environment. I am sure he has noticed that merely laying the blame on individuals because they are gay, sick, alcoholic, fat, mad...etc is not the way forward; society should take more responsibility and make more of an effort to understand these individuals in order to help them. Lastly, I wanted to ask you if you are finally finished with me?'

The professor smiled and said: 'Oh, don't worry, there are some more tests, but you are going to be all right.'

For a moment there was silence, then suddenly the face of the professor started to change. He had metamorphosed into Ali. I told him angrily: 'Hey Ali. I am not your donkey or guinea pig, leave me alone,' and immediately left the room and ran away. While I ran, I said to myself: 'Oh my god, now they have the size of my dick! I hope when they go to manipulate my dick's associates, they exaggerate its size. These bastards only make big accusations though; the only things they are exaggerating are my slightest mistakes or wrongdoings.'

'Ha, ha, ha'

'Damn Voice'

****

64

Part (5)
Nightmares are turning to Dreams/ Fantasies, and Creativities.
(A good enough scenario for a film or play)

One cold but sunny autumn day in London, I saw a group of people gathering in the street. I knew it must be a demonstration or protest. Since I came to the west I have seen lots of demonstrations and protests; each one of them reminded me of a harsh fact in my country of origin. Over there any kinds of protests, no matter how peaceful they might be, are forbidden and brutally suppressed. I went closer to the crowd to find out why they were demonstrating. It was a demonstration in support of refugees and foreigners. When I saw these people, apart from admiration and respect for them, I also felt guilty; their actions reminded me of the horrible situation of thousands and thousands of Afghan refugees, who are living in Iran. I have never been against them, but when I was there myself I never did anything to support them. Now, as a refugee myself, I understand how these people are committed to humanity.

I looked at their faces and said to myself: 'I wish I could paint their eyes, and put the painting in a place where I'd see them every day; it would be a good reminder of civilised society and of these wonderful people who agitate in such a practical way for a better society.'

'Oh, again you're recalling one of your stories, where a musician was hoping to draw the eyes of many good people. You are thinking of your story called *Their Eyes*. Am I right?'

'Yes, you are right, my dear Voice. Do you have a problem with that?'

'Absolutely not.'

Since The Voice reminded me of one of my stories, *Their Eyes*, I thought I had better go to see the river Thames because that river plays a large part in my story. As I got close to the river, it was sunset. I looked at the beauty of the sunset over the river. I knew that the river joins the ocean and then stretches to the horizon. For a second I wished that I could go to the horizon too; maybe this river could take me to the horizon.

'Yes, it will take your dead body to the horizon.'

'Oh, shut up, Voice, and leave me alone.'

At night, I sat on a bench close to a lamp-post, drowned in my thoughts. I don't know how long I'd been sitting there when suddenly I saw Mr H in front of me, looking at the river and whispering: 'I will find you. Daddy won't leave you, tell me where you are?' He now had grey hair and a long beard, and his clothes were dirty.

I went close to him and asked him in surprise: 'Hey Mr H, what are you doing here?'

First he looked at me strangely, and then with a bitter smile said: 'I knew I would find you here.'

'Why were you looking for me? Why are you in this condition? You look like a homeless person. I was also hoping to see you one day, but not like this. Are you still suffering from stress and delusions? I think you should go back to the hospital again. They are going to help you. Look at me, I am much better now.'

'But not everyone gets better. Remember your friend, Mohammed, he never gets better; just gets prescribed more drugs and medication, making him a senseless vegetable.'

'But at least he is safe. Come on, I'll take you. I'll put you in touch with your family; they are going to look after you.'

He looked at me for a few seconds and with a very serious expression said: 'The only person that can help me is you; you should come with me.'

'To where?'

'To the end of the world.'

'Listen to me, Mr H, I am sorry that I involved you in my nightmares, stories and films, but you seriously need professional help.'

He looked at me and asked: 'Did you hear a voice?'

'What voice? I only sometimes hear my own Voice. Actually I don't even hear that, I created it for the sake of the story. What voice are you talking about?'

'My son's voice. He was only 20 when he jumped into this damn river and killed himself. I haven't been a good father to him.'

I looked at his tired and serious face and said: 'Look Mr H, You are talking about one of my stories. You'd better come out of my nightmares and stories. You are damaging your health. Maybe you have decided to act like a method actor and get deeply into the characters, but please forget them.'

'No, you owe me this. You have to come with me to the end of the world and we should go there - maybe we can save Jack, the boy who was butchered by killers; they cut his tongue and ears and gouged out his eyes. I have to rescue Roxana, the Goddess of Beauty, woman of my dreams; I want to be with her, just for a little while. I want to have a last dance with her, even if it is the dance of death.'

I looked at his sad face and told him: 'Please Mr H, you are not well. You are mistaken; you're just talking about my nightmares and stories. Please let me to take you to the hospital.'

He shouted at me: 'No, remember, I was with you in your nightmares, now you should be with me, you owe this to me.'

'Where should we go then? Where is the end of the world?'

'The end of the world is on the horizon. We have to go to the Himalayas. When we get there, first we do some meditation and prepare ourselves, and then we go to the top of a mountain - to the horizon, where the end of the world is, and hopefully we can save Jack and Roxana. I know an old master there who can help us. His name is Shenya; he can teach us how to do the meditation and get ready.'

'But again, Shenya is one of the characters in my story.'

'Don't argue with me. We are going there. We'll have to walk a lot, but we should be there by next spring. We need the spirit of spring as well. You told me that the spirit of spring can work magic, remember?'

'Yes. Now who told you that you have to go to the end of the world?'

'An angel, her name is Helen.'

'Oh, your fellow actress?'

'What are you talking about? Are you still in your films? You had better come out of your imagination; we have a very hard and difficult mission, and we will need to get moving soon.'

For some time we were both silent and looked at the river. Later he said: 'Look at that lamp. Can you see a butterfly close to it?' I looked at the lamp and said: 'Yes, there is a butterfly flying around the lamp.'

Minutes later the butterfly touched the lamp and was immediately killed and fell to the ground.

Mr H looked at the dead body of the butterfly for a second and then drank some whisky from a bottle that he was carrying and started to cry. Through his tears he said: 'It is very strange, isn't it, why butterflies would kill themselves in this way. Maybe Helen is right, she said they want to be in the centre of light and fire. Do you think it's worth it to die like that? Is it worth dying just for a moment in the centre of life's light and fire?'

'I don't know, but I read somewhere that Helen has a phobia, she is afraid of butterflies.'

'That can't be true! She is an angel, and she loves the beauty of butterflies. Butterflies are beautiful, aren't they?'

'Yes, they are. Maybe you're right; you never can rely on news about celebrities.'

'Celebrities? What celebrities? I am talking about Helen, I don't think you have recovered yet, you are still in the world of films.'

'Oh sorry, I thought you were talking about your fellow actress.'

'I told you that you should come out of your imagination; we are about to start on a very real and important mission. Come and drink a little bit of this whisky. It is getting cooler; I wish we were close to a fire. Maybe we could get close to the centre of light and warm up a bit.'

'We also like fire, I mean us Iranians. We even have a special day in our calendar to celebrate fire.'

'Helen also loves fire, she always talks about it.'

'But she is not Iranian. The way we feel about fire is different. I know a beautiful Iranian poem about fire; let me read it to you, it's called 'Love of Fire':

Searing and roaring flames of the sun
Gave birth to the earth
In the glitter of the sun's flames
Earth has evolved
With the flames of this fire
A new way of human life began
Fire that gives warmth
Fire that gives life
Fire that gives love
Only in the light of the fire
Your beautiful eyes appear
Only fire could make your hands and eyes
More searing than itself
And with your kiss
My distraction began. (10)

'Oh this is wonderful, give me a pen and paper, I want to write it down and read it to Helen.'

I gave him a pen and paper and he wrote it down. I told him: 'Mr H, I don't think that it is a good idea to give this poem to Helen, as you know she is happily married, and if your wife finds out, she'll be very jealous.'

'Are you in the world of nightmares and films again?'

'No, I just don't want you to get into trouble.'

'Have you written this poem for a special lady?'

'No, not at all, I wrote it just for the sake of a story, called *Frankenstein of our Century.*'

'It seems you love your own stories.'

'Yes, my fiction is great, perfect for films.'

From midnight the rain started, and we were rained on for some time till I asked Mr H to go somewhere else and find shelter. We were both soaking wet, but he didn't want to go anywhere else; he thought maybe his dead son was going to ask him for help from the depths of the river. After a couple of hours I managed to convince him to go somewhere else so that we could get undercover. We walked to the town centre and stood close to a building to avoid further rain. There was a drainpipe close to us; we stood there for some time, sunk in on our own thoughts until suddenly I noticed that instead of rain, there was blood pouring out of that drainpipe. I wanted to say something to him, but he looked at me angrily and said: 'Are you in your nightmares again? Yes, you must be, look at the blood pouring from this pipe! Could you please stop your nightmares? I have had enough; it seems that pain and blood is everywhere in your nightmares, don't you think that I have had enough? Look at me; look at the state of me! Your nightmares are killing me. Stop thinking of them.' He went into the middle of the street and stood in the rain again, until a few minutes later he came back close to me and said: '**This is not rain; these are particles of my heart that are raining' (11)**

'Do you understand?' Then he brought his face close to my face and started to cry and said: 'Do you understand? This is not rain; these are particles of our heart that are raining.'

I put my hand on his shoulder and told him: 'You shouldn't get deeply involved in my nightmares or films; it is not good for your health.'

'You shouldn't have involved me in them.'

'I didn't! You have accused me several times of involving you in my nightmares; first of all I do not remember sending you an invitation, it was you that wanted to be involved. Secondly, I'm just a victim, like you and millions of others, but if blaming me makes you feel better, carry on, you are welcome! And finally I think the Voice is absolutely right; no one can control or be in charge of their own nightmares; this is happening in reality as well. I just want to say I am on your side and we're both facing the same problems. I wasn't thinking of a nightmare, I really saw blood pouring from that drainpipe. Now come closer, I want to talk a little bit about death; the real ones that I have witnessed.'

'Are you sure that they are not in your nightmares?'

'They have happened in reality and then turned into my nightmares, but if you know the reality, it will help you to fight the nightmares.'

'Okay tell me, but not too much, I need my energy and strength for our mission.'

'Okay, just a couple of examples. Death started to show its face from my childhood. I remember the first death came to one of my neighbours. I could hear the moaning of his wife. Not long after, I noticed the death of another neighbour; I saw a body lying down in a dark room and later on some people put the dead body into a coffin. When they were carrying the coffin they were chanting some religious slogan, which I found very frightening. Another death I witnessed was that of a child. We used to play together; he had a big lump on his neck and from time to time he disappeared. I now think these were times when he wasn't feeling well and had to stay at home or go to hospital. Eventually one day he died, and again some people put him in a coffin and took him away. He was suffering from cancer, and from that time I learned that cancer is a killer. I also witnessed the death of a cat, which was so sad. I still remember how she has shaking her head like a clock pendulum; half of her body was smashed by a car and within a couple of seconds she died with open eyes. Some years later, death came to my grandfather, who was living with us at the time. But the first violent death I saw was at the age of 16 or 17. It was the day of victory during the Islamic revolution. I was in the military high school, and lots of armed people had invaded our school because our stupid commander refused to put his gun down and surrender. Later that day I was passing a drainpipe and saw blood pouring down from it; a soldier had been killed on the roof by the invaders and his blood was pouring down through the pipe.'

'Okay don't tell me any more of your memories, I don't want to know.'

'But remember, you are the one that asked me to write my Bio. I thought since you are an actor, I can present my Bio in this way, so you can participate in it, like research for a new role, almost like method acting. Now you can have a much better understanding and - who knows? - one day you may want to take the role on.'

'Damn you, and your nightmares and films.'

'Would you like me to continue talking about my experiences of death? I have got a lot more to say.'

'No, stop it, I have had enough.'

I looked at his fearful and tired face and said:

I have lived death
With a sorrowful song
Sorrowful

And through a lifetime both long

And exhausting. (12)

He looked at me and shook his head and said: 'I know, you told me before that you were in the war for eight years; it must have been extremely traumatic. Now we had better go back to the river; the rain has stopped and I have to say goodbye to Helen and ask her to look after my son in the river. She is the only one that told me my son is in absolute calm and tranquility. I believe her. Let's go.'

We went back closer to the river. Near a bridge someone was lying on the ground, covered with an old and dirty raincoat. The raincoat belonged to Mr H. We got closer and Mr H woke the woman under the coat and told her to come with us. He explained that first we'd go for a coffee, and then there was something very important that he wanted to tell her. He pointed at me and said: 'This is Mark, he is my friend.' Helen looked at me and only shook her head.

I told her: 'I am very sorry to see you like this, but you are going to be all right.'

'How do you know?'

'I know, because I was the one who created you.'

Mr H shouted angrily: 'What are you talking about? Do you think that you are God? What do you mean by saying you created her?'

'No, I am not God, I am a writer and Helen is one of the characters in one of my stories, *Their Eyes* - that is the name of the story. Look at her eyes. Aren't they beautiful?'

Mr H shouted again angrily: 'Stop it, I won't let you or anybody else take her into any nightmare, do you understand?'

'Yes, sorry, I'd better shut my mouth.'

Helen stood up and drank some vodka from a bottle. Mr H took the bottle from her forcefully and said: 'You should stop drinking this shit, it will kill you! You should give up drinking not only for your own good, but for Jack's sake. Come with me, I want to tell you something very important.'

We went to a coffee shop and sat around a table. When we were drinking our coffee, Helen asked Mr H: 'What is the important thing that you wanted to tell me? Have you heard any news from Jack?'

Mr H stared at Helen's beautiful eyes for a moment and then said: 'I've found someone that can help me find Jack,' and then looked at me and said: 'Here he is. Mark is going to help me to get there.'

'Where?'

'The horizon, at the end of the world. You told me there is such a place, remember?'

'Yes, are you going to the Himalayas?'

'Yes, we are going there today. We should be there by next spring. Mark told me that the spirit of spring is going to help us to save Jack; also we will have the opportunity to do some meditation and get ready for the situation.'

For a moment Helen looked at me and whispered: 'The end of the world, the Himalayas,' and suddenly with a great expression of authority in her eyes and on her face said: 'I am going with you. I have to meet Shenya - my master - and do some meditation. I am going with you.'

Mr H, shook his head in disagreement, and said: 'No. It's too dangerous, and we'll have to travel for a long time.'

'No, I am coming with you; I promise I won't touch the alcohol any more.'

Mr H said sadly: 'What about this river and my son? Who is going to be here for him?'

Helen put her arms around Mr H and said gently: 'I told you, he is safe, you may be able to see him at the end of the world.' Mr H looked at me in surprise and asked: 'Is it possible?'

'What?'

'To see my son.'

I looked at them and said calmly: 'Look. Both of you are living in another world; you are changing my story. This isn't supposed to happen.'

Mr H angrily responded: 'We'll make it happen!'

'Are we God? What are you talking about? You are not even in my nightmares any more; you are dragging me into *your* nightmares.'

Helen softly, with a beautiful smile on her lips, said: 'This is not our nightmares, this is our dream. We are going to see nice people and beautiful nature. You should come with us.' Mr H also said: 'You promised that you'd help me. Now there are three of us.' I looked at them for some time and said: 'Okay, why not? I am ready for another adventure.'

'Oh, you bloody bastard. You just want Helen to be with you, don't you?'

'Shut up, Voice, what are you suggesting? Are you and your agents using your dirty minds again?'

'No, absolutely not.'

'So keep your comments to yourself.'

Suddenly I noticed that Helen was sitting next to me, with a very sad face. She said: 'Who are you talking to?'

'Nobody, a Voice.'

'Oh, Mr H also sometimes talks to a "voice". Don't worry, I will be there for you as well, and I am sure all of us will find a cure and happiness at the end of the world.'

Sometime later, Mr H opened a map and said: 'Look, this is my plan; we have to go from here to the Himalayas. With regard to our limited time, we have to pass cities, forests, mountains and an ocean to get there. We have to walk long distances, but for some other parts of the journey we can hire a car and take trains. We cross the ocean by ship. By my calculation, if we start travelling today, we can be there by spring.'

I asked Mr H: 'Why don't we wait until spring, and then get a flight? It's much easier.'

Mr H with a touch of anger said: 'This is supposed to be an adventure! During this trip, we can purify our souls and bodies and get ready for our final mission.' He looked into my eyes for a few seconds and said: 'We haven't even started yet, but I can see weakness in your face. You should be much stronger than this.'

'Oh, this must be one of these low budget movies, that's why we have to go through all of these hardships. Why should we have to travel for months? Is this some sort of weird actor's preparation exercise? Don't forget that I am not an actor, you are.'

'What? What are you talking about? Have you got lost in your films and nightmares again? We had better start our journey.'

We walked for days and weeks. During the journey, Helen was in charge of almost everything; where to stop, where to sleep, where to eat... talking and being with her was extremely pleasant and I realised that this was the best way to reach the end of the world after all. I gave all my stories to Mr H to read; he was enjoying reading them.

One day we got to a town which was covered in snow. It was surrounded by huge mountains and we could see some people skating on the lake. Helen suggested we hire a car, so we got a car and Mr H became our driver.

After several hours of driving we came upon signs of an accident in the road. Ambulances and police cars were clustered around a car and a lorry. We just saw some blood on the road. Mr H calmly drove past the scene and said: 'It must have been a fatal accident.' A couple of hours later we saw a woman standing in front of a big mirror next to the road. The mirror reflected back the light from our headlights, almost blinding us. When we got closer to the woman and the mirror, we were able to glimpse the woman's eyes for a second and realised that she was crying blood. Stranger still, the mirror showed the image of a man and two children.

Shocked, Mr H stopped the car and said: 'Did you see that? That lady is crying blood and those people are *inside* the mirror. How?' He looked at me and shouted: 'Oh this must be one of your nightmares or stories, isn't it? I told you to stop dragging us into your stories.'

Helen calmly put her hand on Mr H's shoulder and said: 'Calm down, we have to help that woman, she needs our help,' and then she got out of the car. Mr H and I also got out of the car and went closer to the woman. Helen had already started to talk to her and after a few minutes put her arms around her and said: 'We are going to help you, you should come with us.' The woman pointed at the mirror and, distraught, said: 'No, can't you see? I can't leave them, they are my family.' Helen gently said to her: 'They are in the mirror, they are not real.'

'But, this is better than nothing, I have them in my dreams, I am happy with them.'

Suddenly a strong wind took the mirror and hurled it against the rocks of the mountain. The mirror was smashed and the images vanished. After that, the woman started to cry bitterly. Helen hugged her again and told her: 'Don't worry, you can come with us. We are going to the end of the world; we are also looking for our loved ones. You can find your family there, come with us.'

She agreed to come with us, but before she got into the car, we had to fit in all her luggage We ended up having to put some of her stuff on the roof. We found out that the woman's name was Carol - coincidently the same name as one of the characters in a story of mine. She explained that she desperately needed this luggage, because she had to carry lots of different clothes, and that each item of clothing was important to her.

'You slimy bastard, you are collecting beautiful ladies, aren't you?'

'I knew them all already; I was the one that created them, so you'd better shut up, my dear Voice'.

I snapped out of these thoughts to realise to my surprise that both Carol and Helen were looking at me. Helen put her hand on my shoulder and said: 'Don't worry, Mark, everything is going to be all right. We will eventually get to the horizon, to the end of the world. I bet that over there we will be surrounded by absolute beauty, and we'll find tranquility. We need to experience true happiness.' I looked at them and thought to myself: 'So, now I'm travelling with three actors!'

We continued our journey and Helen was a great help to everyone. We had just arrived at a small town and were about to enter a cheap hotel when we realised that two men were slapping and beating a woman. The woman was desperately asking them for something. She was crying but she persisted in asking for what she wanted. She was pushed and slapped several times, but each time she would go back to them and start begging again. Helen and Carol were watching the scene with sadness and disgust when Mr H said to everyone: 'Please don't get involved. She is asking for drugs, and these men are drug dealers.' Carol went up to them and angrily shouted: 'What are you doing? Leave her alone, what kind of men are you?'

One of the men looked at Carol and with a smile on his face said: 'Who are you, honey? It's none of your business.'

Mr H went up to Carol and said: 'Leave it, let's go,' but Carol's face was set and she approached the men again: 'You'd better leave her alone; you know that I will find you'. Both men smiled and one of them said: 'Oh, you are coming for us, I can't wait!'

Mr H said to them: 'We don't want any trouble, we're going now,' and tried to pull Carol back, but Carol pushed him away and went closer to the woman. She was lying on the ground. Carol helped her to stand and then spoke to her: 'Come with us.' The woman said with a cry: 'Could you please give me some money? I am so desperate. I need a fix. Please help me.' Carol gave her some money and she got her drugs from the men and came back to us. Helen asked her name: 'Jolly' she replied. (Again, the name of a character from a story of mine called *Tree of my Memories*) 'I'm sorry. I just had to get a fix'.

'Oh, adding another beauty, ha?'

'Shut up, Voice. Can't you see that she is very upset?'

Suddenly I noticed that everybody was looking at me with surprise. Helen said reassuringly: 'It is all right, Mark; we are going to look after her' and then asked Jolly if she had a place to go. Jolly said no, she didn't have anywhere to go. Helen gently said 'Well, why don't you come with us then? We'll get some rooms in the hotel.' So we got a couple of rooms, one for Mr H and me and one for the women. We all gathered in one of these rooms to talk and eat some food. Jolly went straight to the bathroom to use the drugs she had bought. When she came back she was in a better condition; she thanked every one and wanted to go, but Helen said: 'You don't have anywhere to go. You can stay with us; first we'd better have some food and drink.' When we were eating, Helen asked Jolly: 'May I ask you, how did you get into this state? Don't answer me if you'd rather not, but I have to tell you that I was a drug addict myself and I understand you perfectly.'

Quietly, and with visible sadness, Jolly began: 'It happened shortly after my father's death. I have been involved in drugs and prostitution for years. Several times I've tried to give it up, but every time I've got involved again. After my father's death, I finally found myself getting close to a man. I thought I had found the love of my life, but unfortunately he killed himself. I miss him so much. His name was Arash; he was an immigrant. He was a very good man and he tried to help me, but when he died I got back into this mess. I've got a daughter but I haven't seen her for a long time. I'm so fed up of this so-called "life". I think I should have killed myself along with Arash. But I couldn't'.

'I loved someone too,' said Helen sympathetically. 'We were both involved in drugs, but suddenly I lost him and I don't know where he is now. Anyway, why don't you come with us? We are going somewhere where you can definitely get help; you may even see your father or Arash again. Also, I know some people that can help you to give up the drugs. You should come with us.'

'Where are you going?'

'To the end of the world, to the horizon, to the Himalayas, over there. I know some people that can help you to give up. All of us in here have lost loved-ones; we're going there to find out what happened to our families, friends and lovers. We will help you to get there.'

'Are you sure you want me to come with you? I'd love to; I don't have anything here.'

Helen's face broke into the radiant smile that transformed her as she said: 'Excellent. We will continue our trip tomorrow.'

While Helen and Jolly were talking, Carol went out of the room and came back a couple of minutes later wearing a very sexy dress. She announced: 'I have to go out for while'. Helen asked her: 'Where are you going at this time of night? It's a bit dangerous for a woman like you.'

'Don't worry about me,' replied Carol confidently. 'I'll be back soon,' and as she was leaving asked Jolly: 'Are those men going to be around here? I need to buy more stuff for you because we'll be travelling and you may not be able to get it anywhere else.'

Jolly was amazed: 'Oh, I am so grateful; I can't believe my luck! Suddenly I have found a group of extremely nice people. Okay, let me come with you.'

'No, I want to do it alone. Just tell me where they'll be.'

'Usually where they were when you saw them before. '

Mr H had fear in his voice as he said: 'Carol, where are you going? Let Mark or me come with you, this is very dangerous.'

Carol smiled again and said: 'Don't worry; I'll be back soon.' And she left.

Mr H looked at me angrily: 'You'd better come with me to the other room.' When we'd shut the door, he shouted: 'What are you doing?'

'Me? Nothing. What do you mean?'

'Listen, I've read all of your stories and I know that Helen, Carol, Jolly and even myself are all characters in them, am I right? In your story called *I Played the Death*, Carol is an actress who loses her husband and children in a car accident. She loses her sanity and lives through her old films. In your story she was set on getting revenge on someone who killed her friend who was a prostitute - and look at her now! The reason she carries so many clothes is so she can change into the costumes she wore for her film roles; like the dress she is wearing now. Jolly is also a drug addict and prostitute in your other story called *Tree of my Memories*. Am I right?'

'Yes, but I haven't asked them to appear along our way! I think this is our destiny.'

'Destiny? Destiny my ass! It is you and your bloody nightmares. Now, I am worried about Carol. We should go and find her; she may get hurt or hurt others.'

'Don't worry, she is going to be all right, I know that; I was the one who created her.'

Mr H fearfully asked me to come over to the window and said: 'Look, can you see her? She has a gun in her hand, and pointed at one of those men. Oh my God, she is going to kill him - and then all of us will be in deep shit.'

We could see that Carol had asked the man to strip, and when he was naked, she asked him to run away. The poor man ran for his life, and Carol walked calmly back to the hotel.

Mr H told me that we'd have to be careful; each time Carol suddenly changed her clothes or her appearance it would mean that she was deep in a character she had played in one of her previous films. I asked him: 'Have you seen all her films?' He said: 'No, I've seen some of them but not all of them. If we knew all of her films, we could predict what she was going to do. We're going to be in a dangerous situation all the time.' I told him: 'Everything is going to be all right,' and then we went back to the other room. Carol gave a large quantity of drugs to Jolly and, smiling at our shocked expressions, said: 'Don't worry, people, this is a toy gun. Those bastards deserved to be robbed.' Jolly gave Carol a hug and said: 'Thank you, you are an extraordinary woman. With this amount of drugs I should be all right for a long time.' Helen took the drugs out of Jolly's hand and said: 'I'll look after these for you. I know, and you know, that when we have more drugs we tend to use.more, so I'd better to keep them for you.'

So we continued our journey and several weeks later we ended up in a small town that had a port. We checked into another cheap hotel and Mr H said that we needed to have a meeting. We went to a room and Mr H said: 'We have to take a ship from here. Tomorrow a big ship is coming here, but we have a major problem. We cannot afford to buy tickets; we've run out of money. I have called this meeting to find out if any of you have any money.' Nobody had any money, so I said: 'I knew this was a low-budget film, which is why we ran out of money, but how come all of you so-called "A-List" superstars don't have any money?'

Mr H retorted angrily: 'Mark, are you in your nightmares again? What film? This is real! Tomorrow is our only chance to take the ship and cross the ocean. The next ship doesn't come here till next month, which is too late for us. We have to be on tomorrow's ship, otherwise we'll never reach our final destination in springtime. If we had more time, we could do some temporary jobs and save some money for our trip, but we don't have time.'

Helen calmly took her Oscar statue out of her bag and said: 'You can sell this. You can get good money for this,' Carol also gave her Oscar to Mr H. Jolly, embarrassed, said: 'I'm sorry, I have already sold mine, I was desperate for money,' Mr H told her: 'Don't worry, we are all in this together,' and took an Oscar out of his own bag and said: 'Okay, this is mine. Hopefully by selling them we can make enough money for our trip.'

I told him: 'Mr H, everybody knows that you have won two Oscars, where is the other one? I am sorry that I can't help you with money. I've been writing for many years but I haven't even got a penny for my writing, and so far I have paid several thousand pounds to publish and distribute my books.' Mr H looked at me for some time and then sheepishly admitted: 'Oh, I'm sorry, these trophies are so precious to me.' He then put his second Oscar with the rest of them, and said: 'I am going to sell them and buy the tickets for tomorrow.' He got up and left without another word.

Mr H came back later in the evening, looking dejected: 'Nobody knows what an Oscar is here; they don't even have a cinema! I don't know what we can do.'

Moments later, Carol went out of the room, and after several minutes came back having changed her clothes. She motioned to Jolly to join her as back-up. Mr H looked at Carol and asked: 'Where are you going? What do you want to do?' Ignoring him, Carol asked: 'Is there a bank in this town?'

'No, why are you asking?'

'What about a big supermarket?'

'Yes, there is a supermarket. What do you want to do?'

'Don't worry, leave it to me. Now Jolly had an idea what Carol had in mind and, grinning, said: 'Just give me a minute, I need a fix'. Reappearing from the bathroom a couple of minutes later, she announced: 'Now I'm ready to break in to anywhere; I could fight anyone.'

An hour later, they came back and Carol took lots of money out of her bag and said: 'This should be enough for the rest of our trip,' Jolly also laughingly said: 'Carol is the best, she is a real professional.'

Mr H fearfully asked: 'Did anybody see you?'

Carol replied: 'No, our faces were covered. Don't worry, they have no idea who or where we are.'

Helen said, gratefully: 'I don't know how to thank you; you put your life in danger for the rest of us. I'm glad that we have found each other. We're a good team, and I'm sure we will get to the end of the world safely.'

The next day we boarded the ship and continued our journey. In order to cross the ocean we had to travel for several weeks.

One day, we were sitting drinking outside our cabins. The weather was sunny but the air was cold. While we were talking, Carol went to her cabin and came back wearing a bikini. Surprised, I asked her: 'Oh, don't you feel cold?' She didn't answer me and walked towards the front of the ship, expressionless. Suddenly Mr H said: 'Oh my God, I remember!' I said: 'You remember what?'

'A film that she was in - oh my God, we have to stop her!'

'Why? What happened in the film?'

'She jumped overboard from a ship to rescue her lover. Look, she's about to jump! Hurry up, we must stop her!' And all of us ran towards her. Mr H and I took her arms. Mr H, terrified, was shouting: 'Carol, stop it, you are not in that film!' But Carol cried out: 'Let me go, I have to rescue him.' Mr H yelled: 'No Carol, he is not here!' We had to hold her very tight, and she kept shouting: 'Let me go, he is going to die!'

During our struggle to hold her, she put her hand on her heart and collapsed. I said: 'This must be her heart! She is suffering from heart problems.' Fortunately a doctor appeared and gave her first aid, and the ship's medical crew put her in a medical room. All of us were extremely worried about her, but fortunately several days later she recovered fully.

It took us several weeks to cross the ocean, but eventually we were on our way overland once again, surrounded by the beauty of nature. So we could enjoy it more fully, we decided to walk for a few days. One day, around sunset, we stopped close to a tree in the highlands. We set up our tents, and a couple of us had started to make the dinner. As soon as we stopped, Jolly began to stare strangely up at the tree. Sometime later Mr H came over to me and asked: 'What is wrong with Jolly?' I looked at Jolly; she was opening her arms like a cross and crying blood. Mr H wanted to go and talk to her, but I told him we'd better leave her alone; she was grieving for her lost ones. Moments later she started to move her hands and body calmly and softly, as if she were dancing. The sunset shone through from behind her and her strange but beautiful movements in front of the tree created a spectacular scene. Mr H whispered: 'What is she doing?'

'Dancing; that's the dance of death.'

Minutes later she started to cry loudly and shouted at the tree: 'Why did you kill yourself? Why did you leave me? Even you didn't want me! I am sorry; I couldn't do the things you did. Not only did I fail to kill myself, but I am also still a drug addict. I couldn't give it up; I am still in the dirty world of addiction.'

I told Mr H and the others that a man called Arash who was close to her hanged himself from a tree, which was why she was crying.

Sometime later, Helen and Carol went up to her and took her away from the tree. Mr H looked at me and said: 'Can't you see we're all involved in your nightmares, films and stories? Each one of us is suffering in many ways. Why don't you stop it?'

'Stop what? I am not God and I don't have supernatural powers. I am only a writer. Honestly, I have never wanted to cause anyone any grief, but this is our reality. Real life can be much more brutal and harsh for many people. As a writer, I cannot close my eyes to other people's suffering, and say nothing. I know that I'm not God, a prophet or even someone with lots of power. But if in describing the sufferings of others I can help humanity, then this is something I want to do. I know I'm only human, in need of help with my own failings, but I'm trying. I want to be useful, to be helpful to others.'

Mr H put his hand on my shoulder and said: 'We all want better lives for ourselves and for others, I'm sorry if I sometimes blame you. I guess I am looking for a scapegoat. I promise you that I am doing my best to be more understanding.'

Next day Mr H told me that we'd have to move faster: 'Each one of your characters - I mean us - are having great difficulties, it is hard to

80

make sure everyone is looked-after. We should get to the horizon as soon as possible. I am afraid that any of us could harm ourselves at any moment.

'I agree, we have to find a short-cut, but we don't know this area. One of the other things that we have to consider is that there are definitely dangers and hardships on our way to the horizon; each one of us has to face up to these dangers.'

Mr H's face blazed with anger as he said: 'You have already written about these events that we are going to face, haven't you? Why haven't you told me that there are dangers on the way to horizon?'

'I thought you knew! How did you expect to get to the end of the world without any problems? I thought that you knew this better than anybody! And don't forget that it was your suggestion to go to the horizon, not mine.'

'Okay. We'd better get a move-on then. You should take care of your characters; otherwise we'll all end up dead.'

We continued our journey and as we were struggling up a narrow mountain road one day, a lady came up to us. We presumed she must be one of the locals. She was covering her face with a cloth. Mr H asked her: 'Are you from around here?'

'Yes, I am, and I was waiting for you.'

'What? Did you know we were coming?'

'Yes, I have a contact in London; he is a journalist and he told me that you were coming here.'

Mr H looked at me and asked: 'Is this journalist one of your characters as well?'

'Oh, yes, he is very good at his job, and I think he is in love with this woman.' I asked the lady: 'You must be Annabel – is that right?'

'Yes, I am. Now you'd all better come with me; the villagers have provided you with a place to rest and some food. You must be tired and hungry.'

Helen went up to Annabel and embraced her, and said: 'Thank God! I have found you again. Have you heard any news about Jack?'

'No, he is still missing. But don't worry; I will help you to find him.'

Annabel took us to two small village houses where there was food and drink laid-out for us. We started to have our dinner and when night fell, Annabel uncovered her face. I saw for the first time that she was a real wild beauty. Noticing our curiosity, she said: 'I am sorry. I have to keep my identity secret from the villagers. I don't want the authorities to find out that I am in touch with you.'

'Oh, you thought you'd add another beauty, ha?'

'Shut up, Voice - or would it be better to call you "fucking bastard"?'

Suddenly I noticed everybody staring at me in surprise. Helen put her hand calmly on my shoulder and said: 'It's okay, Mark. Everything is all right.'

'I am sorry, I didn't want to be rude, but sometimes this bloody Voice gets on my nerves. Sorry about that.'

Helen was concerned for Annabel: 'What about your family? Have you heard anything about your son and husband?'

Annabel sadly shook her head and said: 'No, they are still missing'. She lapsed into silence, then after some moments she continued: 'Thinking logically, I know they must have been killed by those bastards, but I don't want to believe that. I've been looking for them for a number of years; I just want to know what's happened to them. I have to find them, dead or alive; that is why I have decided to come with you.'

Mr H spoke gently: 'We're very lucky to have you here. You can be a great help to us. You know this area and you can help us to find a short-cut to our destination. So far it has been a great adventure and a very emotional journey for each one of us. We'd love to get there as soon as possible now.'

'I'll do my best to help you; we are going to continue our journey tomorrow. I've never been to the end of the world myself and, like you, I'm hoping to find out about my loved ones.'

Next day the villagers gave us several horses, so we could continue our journey more easily. We had to allocate one horse just to carry Carol's luggage; she wouldn't leave without it. Also we managed to pick up some binoculars and radio transmitters; now our journey was getting more sophisticated.

After several hours of travel, suddenly Mr H shouted: 'Stop, everybody stop!' He was looking through his binoculars to the other side of the mountain. When we had stopped, he came closer to me and said: 'Have a look at that narrow road opposite us.' I looked at the road and I couldn't believe what I saw; in the middle of the road a woman was buried up to her chest and was surrounded by large stones. Her head was badly injured. She was definitely dead.

We all stood and stared, taking the scene in. I told them: 'She must have been stoned to death; we'd better move on, we should all know by now that there are dangers and hardships on our way.'

Mr H came closer to me and said: 'Who did that? I didn't know such things went on here. I just remember that once you showed me a similar thing in your nightmares, but we were in a different country then. Are we in the Himalayas or in your nightmares?'

'I told you, Mr H, we should prepare ourselves for anything. Travel to the end of the world is not easy; we may enter a parallel world that becomes a real adventure. It is very dangerous, but the reward at the end is so precious and it is going to be a unique experience for all of us.'

Shortly before sunset we stopped to eat and get some rest. When we were eating our food Carol suddenly shouted: 'Look, someone's sitting there!' She was pointing at the top of a mountain in front of us, and sure enough a man was sitting there, on the horizon.

Helen looked through her binoculars and, awestruck, said: 'He is Shenya, he is my old master!' And she started to call him in a strange and loud voice: 'Shenya; Shenya…' The reverberation of her voice was simultaneously terrifying and splendid. Unsettled as we were by this, events were just about to become more harrowing as a moment later Shenya's whole body burst into flames. He was still staring at an unknown horizon. Although all of his body was on fire, he stayed still without moving. How could anybody do that? It was as if the deadly heat of the fire was not bothering him at all.

Now Helen was crying loudly, and we realised we had witnessed a unique way of dying; he didn't move or moan and sat stoically still until the fire killed him. Shenya's death and the sound of Helen's moaning resounding around the hillside affected me deeply. I looked at people in our group and told them:

No one has ever killed himself atrociously
Like this; that he has carried his life. (13)

'Did you see his death? Have you ever seen a death like that? No, never; never…

'Now you know how hard our way to the end of the world, to the horizon, is'.

Mr H managed to get close to Helen and took her in his arms, whispering: 'This is only temporary, you should be strong: we can meet your old master again at the end of the world, and we still have to find Jack.'

Helen fought back the tears and said: 'He killed himself because he knew what is going to happen to Jack.'

'No, that's not true; we still have a chance to find him.'

Helen spoke sadly: 'I think that eastern poet is right; in his poem about the children of the deep he mentioned that:

Swamp of destiny with no compassion in front
 Swears of tired fathers in the back
Curse of impatient mothers in the ears
Without hope and tomorrow in the feast
Children of deep
Children of deep   **(14)**

Helen looked into Mr H's eyes and continued: 'What if that poet is right? What if Jack is trapped in the swamp of destiny and can't see a way out, ha?'

'No, Jack is a very brave boy; he knows how to look after himself. Don't worry, we are going to find him.' Annabel also came up to Helen and said: 'I know that Shenya was like a father to you, but we should be strong and push on to the end of the world. When we get there we can all be with our loved-ones, so we have to get there as soon as possible. It's best that we move right now. In a couple of hours' time we will reach a river and we can stay there for the night.' Moments after we set off, a sharp rain started, but shortly after that the sun again appeared on the horizon. Suddenly Mr H, soaked through, stopped and stared at the distant horizon. All of us drew close to him and I asked him what the matter was and why he had stopped. For some moments he didn't say anything but then pointed at the horizon and in great excitement, said: 'Can you see it? It's a rainbow. Can you see the rainbow?' We all looked at the beautiful rainbow and Mr H shouted at the rainbow and said:

Rainbow,
Rainbow,
Rainbow
Colourful
Beautiful to watch
Arc of love
Smile of an angel
Rainbow,
Rainbow,
Rainbow
Mixture of rain and sun
Messenger of light after a grey rainy day
Splendour of freshness
Short living wonder
Rainbow,
Rainbow,
Rainbow

Don't go quickly
Stay with us longer, forever
Give your colours to our life
Make us free to fly away from darkness
Let us stay with the glitter of happiness
Oh rainbow,
Rainbow,
Rainbow
Stay with us longer, for ever   (15)

We all witnessed the tears in Mr H's eyes and the disappearance of the rainbow.

We moved off again and a couple of hours later got to the river. With Mr H's help I made a small fire. After the day's events, everybody was so sad and fearful. Mr H told us all that each one of us had to stay awake for part of the night and keep guard. He said: 'This area is very dangerous and we need to be vigilant at all times.' I agreed to be the first guard for the night. It had been an eventful day and the moon in the clear sky and the sound of the river were splendidly scary. When I was looking at the river, Mr H came up to me and said: 'Did you hear anything?'

'No, what?'

'From this river, have you heard anything?'

I looked at his sad and anxious face and said: 'Mr H, you are better to go and get some sleep; there is no one in this river.'

'I thought that I heard my son's voice; he was asking for help. I thought maybe my son has also been travelling with us; he was only 20 when he threw himself in that damn river, you know. Maybe he lives in a parallel world; you said at any time we may enter a parallel world. Is it possible that he might be in this river?'

'No, he is not here, but hopefully you will find him at the end of the world.'

Mr H looked at the river silently for some time and turning before he left, said: 'Damn River! It killed my son! He was obsessed with the fake beauty of the river; do you know what he wrote on his suicide note? He wrote:

Chilly and silent face of the river
Asked me for a kiss.   (16)

He looked at the river again for several more minutes and than went back closer to the fire and sat next to Helen. Helen was staring sadly into the flames; I looked at them, and asked myself: 'How is getting to the end of the world going to help us? What are we hoping to find there? Can we possibly find the answers to our problems, or be reunited with those we love? How? All of them are dead. Are we all going to die too? I haven't been able to find any logic in our journey. It was Mr H who thought coming to the horizon – the end of the world – was a good idea in the first place. But he lives in a paranoid world himself! How could he possibly know whether getting to the horizon would be the key to a better life? No, it just doesn't add up.'

The next morning Jolly came up to Mr H and me before we got moving and said: 'There is something important that I have to tell you'. Mr H asked: 'What?'

'I think Helen used some of my drugs last night. She was keeping them for me, but because of yesterday's events, especially Shenya's death, she was in a situation she couldn't deal with, so she has started to use drugs again. One of you should talk to her and take the drugs away from her.' Mr H nodded his head sadly and said: 'Thanks for letting us know. I am going to talk to her and take the drugs away.'

He asked Helen to go with him, some distance away from the others, and moments later we could hear the bitter argument between them. Sometime afterwards they rejoined the rest of us, and Mr H asked Annabel: 'Where is that place for meditation? I have heard there are some people over there who are helping people with addiction. We are all tired, and I think that it might be a good place to rest.' Annabel responded: 'Yes, I know where that place is. I will take you there. It is a beautiful and very peaceful place and we can all relax and have a rest. It will take us a day's walk to get there, so if we move now we can be there this evening.'

So we arrived that evening. Nestled in the hollow of a huge mountain, it was a very beautiful place. Now it was the beginning of spring, and wild flowers were scattered all over the mountain. We were welcomed by some very kind people and we also met the Wise Man, who was very welcoming. Over the days that followed we all regularly participated in meditation. The relaxing atmosphere and the meditation were very useful to all of us, and after a few weeks we all felt much better. Helen and Jolly, both with strong willpower and with the help of counselling and meditation, managed to give up drugs and both looked much better.

On the day before we were due to start our journey again, the Wise Man asked us to have a meeting with him. He said: 'I know where you are going. I should warn you that there is still more danger and difficulty on your way; from the time you first arrived, I have been monitoring each one of you, watching your spiritual progress. You have all suffered massively. My advice to you is, when you manage to pass the barriers and get close to the horizon, only one of you should go to the exact location. He or she can reflect the spirit of spring and the Goddess of Beauty for the rest of you. That person must not only have the greatest desire to reach the end of the world, but also have the highest spiritual power amongst you. That person is going to have a great responsibility. I can suggest one of you, but it is totally up to you, you are the ones who have to choose that person.'

I asked him: 'Who do you suggest?' The Wise Man calmly replied: 'Based on my observations from the time you arrived, I think Mr H is the best person for the purpose.'

Mr H said: 'Oh no! Why me? There are others that are stronger than me, both physically and spiritually.'

The Wise Man replied: 'That is my decision, and if I am not mistaken, you were the one who came up with the idea of travelling to the Horizon, which shows you have the greatest desire to go there. Also I have noticed that you look after everyone and have shown good leadership.'

I said: 'Yes, he was the first to suggest going there and during our journey he has been so caring towards everyone. I agree with the Wise Man. He is the one that should go.' Everybody agreed with the Wise Man's suggestion.

The next day we continued our journey. For security reasons we decided not to enter any village on our way, so after a couple of days' travelling we came one afternoon close to a village, but went to the top of a nearby mountain instead. We had just arrived on top of the mountain when suddenly the village and all the surrounding area came under attack by shells, missiles and bullets. We could see that the houses of the villagers were targeted. Men, women and children were running away from their homes and trying to hide and find shelter on the mountain. It was a very shocking scene. Sometime later, first some local spies entered the village and started looting and setting fire to some houses, and an hour later military forces entered the village and destroyed all the houses with explosives, arrested some of the villagers and stole all the domestic animals - cows, sheep, and so on. Overnight, the whole village was on fire. Some of the villagers who had managed to escape came to us; they were all crying and mourning for their lost ones. Some of them had lost members of their family. It was a nightmarish situation.

Mr H came to me and said: 'It is you again, ha?' I said: 'Possibly. I witnessed a similar thing in reality, maybe it's happening again. I have never forgotten that event; some bastards attacked and set fire to an entire village, exactly like this. It was one of my hardest and saddest times on that mountain.'

'Which mountain?'

'In Kurdistan. I witnessed a similar event there. The Iraqi army did the same thing with the help of local spies.'

'Damn you, we are not in Kurdistan any more. These things don't happen here! We must be in your nightmares; we must have entered a parallel world, mustn't we?'

'Yes, I think so; our situation gets more and more dangerous.'

Mr H started to talk into his radio transmitter; he was explaining our position to someone over the radio. I asked him: 'Who are you talking to?'

'To my associates, I am trying to get some help.'

'Who are your associates?'

Frowning, Mr H commented: 'You think that I don't know anybody. I have lots of connections in high places.'

'Where? In Hollywood? How can they help?'

'Listen; from the time I accepted responsibility for the group, I've done my best to carry on our mission. As I told you, I have connections with some powerful people who can help us. Now please leave me, I have to talk to people.'

I went up to Helen and Jolly. They were both trying to help the villagers. I asked them where Carol was. Nobody knew where she was, so I looked around and eventually found her; she was in a military uniform. She must have played a role in a war movie before, which was why she *had* a military uniform. I went up to her and asked: 'What are you doing?'

'What does it look like? I am ready for a fight; we should defend ourselves and the villagers.'

'With what? You just have a military uniform, nothing else; we don't have any weapons! We should stay away from them.'

'But we can get some of their weapons; we have to trap and attack a small number of them, and get their weapons.'

Sometime later Mr H approached and said to Carol: 'Oh Carol, please don't do anything stupid. We cannot start to fight the army. We have to get to the horizon as soon as possible; getting there is the only chance that we have. We have to move immediately.'

We set off again, and some old men, women and children from the village also came with us. One of the villagers told us that the 'base of evil' was there: 'Those military men came from there to destroy our village.' Mr H asked: 'what do you mean? What is this base of evil?'

'It is a big base in a mountain valley; those military men and bomb squads were from the base of evil. They've been carrying out these brutal attacks for many years, You should be very careful; if they capture you, you will be tortured and then executed. They are so brutal.'

We travelled all night and in the morning came close to a village. We decided to go to the village and get some food and rest. On our way I saw Mohammad. I couldn't believe that Mohammad was there; he was wandering around and lost. I walked up to him and asked: 'Hey Mohammad, what you are doing here?' He just looked at me strangely and didn't say anything. I said again: 'Mohammad, it's me, Mark, do you remember me? I'm your friend, why are you here?'

He said: 'Yes, I remember you. How are you, my friend? Nice to see you. I am glad that you found me. I was lost - it's my wife's fault. She was the one that asked me to come here. She was sitting on the back of a dragon and gave me a lift to get here, but I don't know where she is now. I think she has gone to see an evil person. All the bad people in this area know her, I think she is a criminal herself. Last night she put a knife to my throat and cut my head off, and then she whispered some magic words and glued my head back on to my body.'

Mr H came up to us and said: 'Mohammad, what are you doing here? Do you remember me? We were in the same hospital.'

'Oh yes, I remember you. I am glad that you can talk now. When you were there, you didn't talk to anyone. It was as if someone was biting your tongue and that was why you couldn't talk. For me, it was as if someone was betting on my brain; that was why I couldn't think. Maybe it was black magic, I don't know.'

'What are you doing here?'

'I just wanted to sleep with a prostitute in a whorehouse, but they wouldn't let me in. I don't go there any more; there are lots of bad people there. You shouldn't go there either.'

I said to him: 'Mohammad, you have been lost; I don't know how you got here, but don't worry, we will ask a nice person in the village to look after you. We have to go somewhere; we will be back and take you home.' We took him to the village and asked a family to look after him for while.

Mr H came to me and said: 'It is you again, ha? How did Mohammad get here?'

'I don't know, but like the other villagers he was talking about evil people and a brothel; I think we're still in Kurdistan. Remember that old man was also talking about the base of evil; we'd better gather more information about the area before we go, and also we should leave the village as soon as possible. There are lots of spies here; they are going to report us to the base of evil. We should pretend that we are just passing; we shouldn't tell anybody where we are going.'

Several hours later, we moved out of the village. Annabel had been able to gather useful information from the villagers. She told us: 'We could get to the horizon in one day, but the problem is we have to pass the base of evil and they've laid mines all over the area. The commander of the base is a well known bastard; he is a sick sadistic son of a bitch.'

We found a small cave at the top of a high mountain. It was a good place for us to stay, and the cave was concealed behind a big tree, so nobody could see us. We decided that first some of us should get close to the base and monitor the situation and hopefully find a safe way to pass by, and then we should all move together towards the horizon.

Mr H said to all of us: 'I think it is better that Mark, Annabel and I go to recce the situation around the base and hopefully find a way to pass it, then come back here for the rest of you.'

Carol's face took on a determined expression as she said: 'I am coming with you.' Mr H calmly replied: 'Carol, this is real, we are not in any war film. The situation is extremely difficult and dangerous. Annabel comes with us because she knows the way.'

'You think I don't know our situation? I am coming with you, and I can be as good as you or Mark or Annabel.'

'I know that you are brave, but I don't want you do something that jeopardises our mission, now we are so close to our goal.'

'I promise that I won't do anything stupid, and I will follow your orders.'

Mr H nodded his head and said: 'Okay, but remember you have promised to listen to me.' Then he told Helen and Jolly to stay behind and be careful, and not to contact anybody. He explained that we should get there by tonight, and we would be back again by tomorrow.

We kept moving all day and at midnight reached the top of a mountain. Now we could see the base clearly: it was a large circular compound and was surrounded by an embankment and several military guard-posts.

We stayed for some time, searching everywhere for a safe passage, but all the ways and paths were blocked by barbed wire and mines. It seemed that the only safe passage was through the base itself. We were looking at the base and the area around it when suddenly some military men brought two captives out of a building. They were both handcuffed and their heads, faces and feet were covered in blood and bruises. They must have been tortured severely. The military men took their two

90

prisoners close to a fire and started to beat them again; moments later, the prisoners were lying bleeding. The military men went back into their shelter and left them there.

We all watched these scenes with a sense of horror and shock. Some time later we saw one of the prisoners stand up, go close to the other and say something to him. Seconds later the second prisoner also got up, and both of them started to dance. How could they do that? Both of them were bleeding heavily; they were especially badly bruised on their feet, but they carried on dancing.

I said to Mr H, Annabel and Carol: 'Look at them, they are dancing the dance of death. Look at them, you can't see such a thing anywhere else in the world.' Soon some military men came back and savagely beat the prisoners again, and then put them close to the embankment, and at the order of the commander of the base, shot and executed them.

We couldn't believe what we were witnessing. I said:

No one ever killed himself atrociously
Like this; that they have carried their life   (17)

Mr H fearfully asked me: 'Who were those prisoners?'

'Seerous and Taher, they were both political prisoners. They were two characters in my very first novel, *The Last Scene*.'

'So it's you and your nightmares again ha?'

'This is what they do: torture and execution.'

Again some military men brought another body out of the same building and put him next to the bodies of the prisoners. With fear and fury in her voice, Annabel said: 'Oh my God, that is Jack. They've killed him too. Look at his face! They cut off his ears and tongue, and gouged out his eyes.' It was another extremely harrowing scene.

I whispered: so he was right; the eastern poet, when he wrote about the children of deep:

Swamps of destiny with no compassion in front   (18)

Jack also had faced his destiny; been killed atrociously by torturers.

Mr H's shaky voice broke through the silence: 'That's enough. We'd better go back. We were about to leave when Carol said: 'Hey look, they are bringing out more bodies.' This time they brought the bodies of a man and a boy and put them close to the rest of the dead. Annabel sadly acknowledged: 'These two are my husband and my son.' We were all shocked. Carol put her arms around Annabel. Mr H, with tears in his eyes, said to me: 'That is enough; we have seen enough of your nightmares.'

'These are things that happened in reality, these are not my nightmares.'

Sometime later we saw that a bulldozer was digging a grave and later on the military men put all the dead bodies in that grave.

We all had a terrifying night; it had been very shocking to see those scenes. Annabel was in a terrible state. She couldn't even cry; her face was like a statue of sadness and revenge. She was painfully silent. After moving away from the evil base, Mr H asked us to stop and said: 'Annabel, I don't know what to say, it was a terrible scene for all of us, but it has been much harder for you. I am so sorry for your loss; I wish there was a way that we could help you. It is a difficult time, on the one hand losing our loved-ones and on the other not to be able to find a way to our final destination. I don't know what we do now, but I can promise that I'll do my best to get some help and find a way to the horizon.'

Carol said in despair and sadness: 'How? How could you find a way to get there? There is only one way to get there; passing through the middle of that damn base.'

Mr H calmly responded: 'I know, at the moment it seems impossible, but you never know, we may find a way. I am going to contact my friends. They might be able to help us.'

Annabel angrily said: 'Who do you think you're kidding? Nobody can help us; we have to solve our problems by ourselves. So far during our journey, we have managed to overcome all obstacles. This is the last one and we have to do it by ourselves.'

Mr H asked: 'Do you have any plan?'

'Not yet, but I am not going to give up. No, never! These bastards have to pay for their brutalities. I have waited for years; I have cried almost every night, and it is not only me: I know lots of other people in more or less similar situations to my own; some of them are even worse than that. No, I am not going to give up.'

For some time there was a bitter silence among us, then Mr H said: 'You have every right to be angry and vengeful. I am not going to give up, either; I don't think any of us are going to give up. But we should be careful - we are not in a position to start a war. We should be patient. There must be a way to pass these bastards. I want to ask you something else: I think we shouldn't say anything about Jack and his death to Helen.'

Annabel said seriously: 'Why not? Why do you want to give her false hope? She should know what has happened.'

'We are in a dangerous situation; I don't want her to lose it again. She is a very vulnerable individual and has gone through a lot, maybe in future and when we are in a better situation we can tell her, but not now: we just tell Helen and Jolly that our way is blocked by these evil people.'

We got back to our base the next morning. Helen and Jolly realised that there was a problem just by seeing our faces. Helen calmly asked: 'Did you get there?' Mr H said: 'Yes, but all the paths are blocked by the enemy. We must find some way to get past - don't ask me how, I don't know yet, but I am working on it.'

Several hours later Mr H said: 'I have to go somewhere, I have managed to contact some people, I have to go and see them. They are about one day's walk away from us. Hopefully they can help us; I will be back in a couple of days. I leave Annabel in charge of our group. You shouldn't go anywhere; if you need anything, Annabel can help you. She knows the area and the local people.' Mr H took one of the horses and was about to set off when I went up to him and said: 'Where are you going? Who do you want to see?'

'I've told you, I am going to see some people.'

'Oh, things moving away from my nightmares and stories ha?'

'They'd better be! All of us have had enough of your nightmares. We have to do something about this situation. Take good care of the women; all your so-called "characters" are in a terrible position,' and with that he left.

I was so tired that I went straight to sleep. Several hours later, I woke up to find another woman in our camp. Jolly came to me and said: 'How do you feel now? Are you still tired?'

'I am okay, who is she?'

'Oh, that is Maria, she is Annabel's friend. Don't worry she is a very close friend of hers.'

'But we have to be careful! If these bastards found out about us, they would come for us, and we wouldn't be able to defend ourselves.'

I went out of the cave and found Annabel, Carol, Helen and Maria sitting close to a fire next to the tree. Annabel introduced Maria to me and said: 'She is my friend and a member of the resistance. She and her comrades have been fighting against these evil insurgents for years.' I wanted to talk to Maria but Annabel said: 'She can't speak English, she only speaks Spanish.' I went up to them and sat next to the fire. Now it was night and the moon shone in a clear sky. Annabel and Maria went to the cave to continue talking. Jolly sat next to me and said with a big smile: 'Oh, come on, cheer up, it's not the end of the world. Eventually we will find a way.' I responded with a bitter smile: 'I know it's not the end of the world! That is exactly our problem: we can't get there.'

Carol asked: 'Do you think we'll be able to find a way to get there?'

'I don't know, I hope so, but you have seen the problems.'

'You think Mr H and his contacts can help us?'

'I have no idea; I don't know who his contacts are.'

'I wish I could see my family one more time. If I see them again, I won't let them leave without me. That's the only reason I keep going.'

I looked at her sad and beautiful face and said quietly: 'I know it is very hard for you to believe, but your children and husband have already gone. You should accept the truth; we must all accept the harsh reality that all our loved-ones have gone. '

'So, why are we here then?'

'To be honest, I don't know what Mr H's idea was; he is the one who believes that by getting there we can all find purpose and happiness in our lives. I have no idea what is going on at the end of the world. Let's just hope that we get there.'

Sometime later we all sat close to the fire and had some food and drink. Afterwards I said to Jolly, who was sitting next to me: 'Look at the moon. See how beautiful the moonlight and all this nature is - not just beautiful, but splendidly scary as well.' Jolly stared at the tree for some time and then said: 'Yes, I agree with you, it is splendidly scary. Do you know what this tree reminds me of? It reminds me of my friend Arash. He hanged himself from a tree; he died with a smile on his lips.'

Moments later Helen said: look what Maria gave me; it is a book of poems. It has an English translation too. It's by a poet called Lorca; he was a great poet, but fascist bastards killed him. We all had a look at the book and Helen read some of his poetry to us. Some time later Annabel said: Maria is a very good singer, I asked her to sing a song for us. She is going to sing a song about the moon. It is a song written by Lorca. Now we must listen to her. Maria started to sing; she had a very powerful voice:

Ballad of the moon, the moon

The moon came to the forge
wearing her bustle of bulbs.
The boy's looking at her,
looking and looking
in the disturbed air
the moon moves her arms,
and lewd and pure, lifts
her hard metallic breasts.
Run, moon, moon, moon
If the gypsies come,

They will make necklaces, white rings
out of your heart.
Child, let me dance
If the gypsies come
They will find you on the anvil,
Your bright eyes closed.
Run, moon, moon, moon,
I hear their horses now.
Leave me, child, don't trample
My starched whiteness
     ***
The horseman came nearer
drumming across the plain.
Inside the forge the child's
Eyes are tight shut.
Through the olive-grove they came,
Gypsies, bronze and sleep,
Head high,
their eyes behind their lids.
     ***
How the barn-owl sings,
How it sings in the tree!
The moon goes through the sky
Holding a child's hand
Inside the forge the shouting
Gypsies weep.
The air maintains its watch,
Watching, watching.   (19)

We spoke and chatted for several more hours. When I went back to the cave to go to sleep, I heard a sad moaning voice. I came back out, and Jolly with tears in her eyes said: 'Don't worry, it is Carol, she is very emotional, let her cry. I think she is thinking of her dead children and husband.' Her sad voice reflected back from the mountains that surrounded us, sounding both sorrowful and spectacular in the moonlit night. It touched the very depths of our souls, reflecting our lives too. That voice expressed nothing but pain, sorrow and death.

Next day Annabel went to the village again with Maria, but only Annabel came back in the evening. She told us that there was a way to get to the Horizon, but it was very dangerous: 'I have spoken to Maria and some other members of the resistance; we have a plan, I am waiting for Mr H to come back so we can discuss the plan with him. It isn't just us who've got to deal with those bastards; sooner or later the villagers and the resistance will have to confront them, too, but it is going to be very dangerous.'

Jolly burst into a smile and said: 'Oh my god, are we going to fight? I can't wait to kill some of these bastards!'

Helen said calmly: 'Jolly, you don't know what you're talking about. Fighting and war is not easy; none of us is trained for fighting. How can we fight?'

'Look at me, what have I got to lose?' said Jolly, seriously. 'Learning about guns can't be too difficult. We can learn from Maria and members of the resistance.'

Helen responded: 'We are in the middle of spring and we don't have time for training and going to war. We are not professional soldiers.' Carol said: 'I had training before.'

Helen said patiently: 'But your training was for films, here we are in the real world.'

Annabel said: 'We are not going to stay here for long; we have a plan for a rapid action, and quick victory. If everything goes according to plan, we should be able to destroy them in a couple of days. You should learn how to use a gun and hopefully you are not going to use it at all.'

The next morning, Mr H came back. We all looked anxiously at his face, but we could tell by his sad expression that his contacts hadn't been any help. For a couple of moments I looked from his sad, disappointed face to the women with their bitter silence, and I whispered:

In the lead's background of the morning
Horseman
Has silently standing
In the wind, long mane of his horse
Has dishevelled
God, God
Girls shouldn't be silent
When men
Hopeless and tired
Are getting old   (20)

Later on, Annabel talked to him and explained her plan. Mr H asked us to have a meeting; when we were all gathered he said: 'I went to see some people who I thought might be able to help us, but I was wrong. I think the only option is to go ahead with the plan worked out by Annabel and the resistance. They have a good plan; I will talk to you about it tomorrow. We are going to move closer to the village.'

Next day before we left, Mr H explained the plan. He said: 'Annabel and Maria have managed to get jobs in a brothel. Carol, Jolly and Helen: you are going to join them. One night a week, a lorry full of these bastards comes to the whorehouse. We, with the help of the resistance, are going to eliminate them and then pack the lorry with explosives and take it back to their base. The power of the explosives should be enough to wipe out the entire base. Immediately after the explosion, all of us will enter their base and then go towards the horizon. After passing the base we are going to be close to the end of the world; each one of you just needs to know how to use a gun.'

Smiling knowingly, Jolly said: 'This is easy; I know very well how to play a prostitute. I am good at it! It was my previous job.' Carol also said: 'Piece of cake, easy for me as well.'

We all went to the brothel; there were another five working girls there. Mr H and I pretended that we didn't know anybody and that we were just there for pleasure. Helen, Carol, Annabel and Jolly wore very sexy dresses. Annabel came to Mr H and whispered: 'One of these working girls has already given the news of the arrival of new girls to the base of evil. Tonight there will be more of them than usual coming here; they want to see the new girls. I have already prepared a strong sleeping drug in some bottles of wine, so each one of them should fall fast asleep after drinking a glass of wine and then the members of the resistance will deal with them.'

In the evening all of us gathered in one room. Mr H was hiding a knife and a gun underneath his clothes, and said: 'Have you hidden the guns properly?' Everybody checked their guns. Mr H said again: 'In the last couple of hours you have all learned how to use a gun, but we should do our best not to use them. I think between 15 to 20 men are coming here tonight. Each of you has to take them one by one to your room and give them contaminated wine. We will also try to give the same wine to the men in the main hall. Just remember they are all professional fighters and all of them carry guns. The soldier who will be driving the lorry is a member of the resistance. When all of them are here, the lorry will be packed with explosives. One major problem and danger is that when we try to take the lorry back into their base without the rest of the soldiers, the guards may get suspicious, so our plan is that the driver, Annabel and Mark will go back to their base. The only good thing is that the lorry will be going back there in the very early morning and apart from the guards the rest of the soldiers will be asleep. Only the two guards in the entrance are a problem; hopefully

Annabel can distract them until the lorry gets parked and then Mark, the driver and Annabel will come out. This is our plan so far, but you never know what is going to happen. Are there any questions?'

Helen said ruefully: 'I don't think I would be able to kill anybody.'

'Don't worry, I will be with you all the time,' Mr H reassured her. 'You don't have to do anything, just pretend that you are a working girl and I am your client for the night. We all know that you are under severe stress; we will work as a team. Now all of you had better go to the main hall. They'll be here soon.'

When the girls went out of the room, I said to Mr H: 'Why didn't you tell me before that I have to go with that lorry?'

Mr H looked at me seriously: 'You are the best person to go there; Annabel needs a reliable back-up.'

'But I am just a writer.'

'Don't forget that you have already been in the army.'

I looked at Mr H and I closed and opened my eyes several times. He said: 'What is wrong with your eyes?'

'Nothing. Sometimes you look like Ali or Mr Smith, and I feel like a donkey.'

'What are you trying to say?'

'Why not *you*? Why don't you go there? You just picked up the best job in the world – looking after beautiful Helen – and sending me to hell, ha?'

'Look, I am an actor, I haven't trained to fight; you are the best man for this job - and don't forget I have a much more important mission to accomplish. I am the only one who has to go to the horizon. I am a messenger. Don't worry, Annabel is very brave. She is going to look after you. We'd better go to the main hall now. We'll just stay in a corner; don't talk to any of them. If somebody wants to talk to us, we just pretend that we are totally drunk, because we don't know their language.'

Several hours later, a lorry full of the military men arrived and 18 military men came inside the house. Annabel, Carol, Jolly and Helen welcomed them, smiling. Looking at them, I said to myself: 'Well done, Mark. Look how beautiful the characters from your stories are.'

'And how fucking horny you are.'

'Oh fucking Voice - with that dirty mind again!'

Mr H interjected: 'Who are you talking to? Is that Voice again? Please concentrate, we are in a very dangerous situation, it is not a good time to talk to The Voice.'

'Sorry, it is not me that wants to talk to The Voice. The fucking Voice comes and goes whenever it wants. Okay, I am going to concentrate one hundred percent.'

Jolly, Carol and Annabel took their first victims to their rooms with great professionalism and, after ten minutes, each one of them came out and signalled to Mr H that things were going well. Helen was close to Mr H and pretending that she was with him, and some members of the resistance immediately took the unconscious bodies out through the back door.

Jolly, Carol and Annabel did the same thing once more, which left only twelve soldiers in the hall. Some of them were completely drunk. Around midnight, we suddenly heard shooting from Annabel's room. For a second everybody froze. First, Jolly came out of her room, immediately jumped on a table and - in order to distract the soldiers from the shooting – launched into an erotic dance. Moments later, Annabel came out of her room with two members of the resistance and started to shoot. Carol also came out and began shooting soldiers, and then Jolly excitedly joined in, too. Within seconds, all the soldiers were dead. It was an unbelievable scene; Helen was hiding herself in the arms of Mr H. She didn't want to see the killing.

Sometime later Mr H went up to Jolly and said: 'Hey, Jolly, come down, they are all dead.' Jolly jumped down and went up to Annabel and said: 'Oh my god, you're a sharp shooter,' and then looked at Carol and said: 'You too! Oh my god, we've killed all of them.'

Mr H asked Annabel: 'Why did you start to shoot?'

'Because that bastard in my room didn't want to drink the wine, he wanted to have sex first.'

Mr H told me that I should change my clothes; there was a soldier's uniform in the lorry for me and the lorry was already packed with explosive.

I went out and changed my clothes and Annabel, the driver and I moved off towards the base. The driver told me that when we got there I'd better pretend to be totally drunk and stay inside the lorry. Annabel was going to keep the guards busy and the driver would park the lorry inside the base. We would then go back to Annabel to get rid of the guards and, twenty minutes after parking the lorry, it would explode. We would then have time to join the rest of the members of the resistance outside the base and we would invade the base immediately after the explosion.

We got close to the entrance of the base and two guards came to check the lorry. One of them asked the driver where the others were. The driver smiled and said: 'You haven't heard the news?'

'What news?'

'There are several beautiful new girls in the whorehouse; everybody is busy there,' Then he looked at Annabel and said: 'See, I brought one of them for you. You have only fifteen minutes, because I have to go back to get the rest of the soldiers, okay?'

The guard said excitedly: 'Oh you are the best man in the entire world!' Annabel got out of the lorry and took the two guards into a corner and started kissing them. The lorry driver took the lorry inside the base, parked it close to the commanding officer's building and set the timing-device attached to the explosive. When we both got back to Annabel, the two guards were lying dead. Annabel had managed to kill them both with a sharp knife. I looked at Annabel; she was truly a symbol of revenge. We got out of the base and joined the rest of the members of the resistance. We waited for the massive explosion and then we all invaded the base. Explosions killed almost everyone on the base except a couple of soldiers, and they were arrested by members of the resistance.

We stayed at the base for some time while Mr H was trying to find the best way to the horizon. The smell of gunpowder and death pervaded the air. Carol, Jolly, Helen and I silently watched the devastation. Members of the resistance were collecting guns and documents from the base. Eventually Mr H came to us and said: 'Okay, I was talking to some members of the resistance and I asked them about the way to horizon. Now I've got good information. I think we should move now. By my calculation we are going to be there this evening.' Than he asked where Annabel was. I told him she was at the corner of the base; she was next to the mass grave.

Helen in fear and surprise asked: 'Why she is there? Did she find her family?'

'I don't know, but the resistance have found a mass grave over there.'

Helen went up to Annabel. Annabel was staring at the grave. Helen said gently to her: 'What has happened? Why are you here?' Annabel said, without looking at her: 'I need some time to be with my family.' Then she lay down on the grave and put her face to the ground. Mr H went and stood next to Helen and said quietly: 'Let her be on her own; come with me.' Annabel was whispering something in her own language; she was probably saying farewell to her loved-ones. Sometime later she started to cry. Carol, Jolly and Helen were also in tears. It was the first time Annabel had been able to cry since witnessing the death of her family. I whispered:

Let me cry like clouds in the spring

Stone groans
On the day of lovers' farewell   (21)

Sometime later, Annabel got up, wiped the tears from her face and then came to us and said: 'Okay, here is my final destination. I have found my family; they are all dead.' Mr H said, sadly and calmly: 'No, here is not your final destination, I have found the exact way to the horizon, and we can be there this evening.'

'To do what? Let me ask you a question: what is in that bloody place? What can we find there?' And then she pointed at the mass grave and shouted: 'That's *it* - that is the reality. They are all dead and we can do nothing about it. They are all dead; dead; dead, do you understand? Why don't you stop your obsession? Up there on the horizon there is nothing; why do you give these people false hope?' She then looked at Helen and said: 'Jack is dead, and nobody can bring him back,' Turning to Carol, she said: 'It is the same thing for your family.' To Jolly, she said: 'Arash is dead.' And finally she stared at Mr H: 'Your son, also, is dead; dead; dead.' She started to cry again: 'Why don't you want to accept the reality? They are all dead.'

Mr H with tears in his eyes said: 'Calm down, please. We are so close to the end of the world. After all this hardship that we've been through, we are very close to our final destination. You have no right to end your journey here. I won't let you stop here. Just one more day and night, what have you got to lose? Just one more day, remember what the wise man said? He said that you are going to have a very difficult journey, but it's worth it to try. Now we are almost there. You should come with us; this also gives you the opportunity to prove me wrong.' I said: 'We all should try. Although I am more in agreement with Annabel, so far we have acted as a team. Let's finish it: we have nothing to lose.' Jolly also said: 'Yes, I agree, just one more day, we should all go there.'

Mr H went and stood in front of Helen and told her: 'Now you have heard the bad news, now you know that Jack is dead, I want you to promise me that you are not going to harm yourself.' Then he looked at Carol and Jolly and said: 'You should all promise that you are not going to harm yourselves. I know in my heart that there is something special at the horizon, that is why we have all survived so far - that must tell you something. I believe somehow we are protected by a powerful force, maybe by the spirit of spring or Roxana or God. Now are you with me or not? Just for the next 24 hours, that is the only thing I am asking.'

After some moments of silence, everybody accepted that they would follow Mr H. We took some food and drink and moved off towards the horizon on our horses. As we rode, Mr H came close to me and said: 'I don't want any more of your nightmares. We have all had enough. I have read all your stories; are we expecting more nightmares?'

'No, from now on, you are in charge. I just have one unfinished story. That is a story about the Second World War and the resistance in France. I don't know when I will be able to finish that story. As I said before, from now on you are in charge totally. I hope that you know what you're doing. Personally I don't believe that we'll see anything special up there.'

'Don't be so pessimistic, I am sure we will experience something unique.'

In the evening, Mr H pointed at the top of a mountain and said: 'There, over there, can you see it? We are going to get very close to it and then you'll stay, and I'll go to the top first. We should be there in half an hour.'

Several minutes later, suddenly three armed men appeared from three different directions and commanded us to stop. We were all shocked as we weren't expecting to be trapped by anybody. Mr H asked them: 'Who are you and what do you want?' One of them said: 'We were in that base that you destroyed. We managed to escape; now it's pay-back time.' They were about to shoot us when suddenly we heard gunfire and the men collapsed one after another. Immediately, Mr H shouted: 'Let's go, we should go at once!' Annabel wanted to check the dead bodies, but Mr H shouted again: 'Let's get away from here, there may be more of them. We should get to the horizon as soon as possible.' We moved on again and Mr H called out: 'Did anybody see who shot the men?' Nobody knew who had done it. Suddenly Annabel exclaimed: 'Hey, look at the horizon!' We all looked over. For seconds there was a light, like moonlight, at the horizon, which then disappeared. Mr H shouted again: 'Let's go.' We moved on and came to a tree near the horizon. Mr H asked everybody to dismount from their horses and said: 'Here we are very close to the horizon, you can see it from here clearly. From here, I am going to the top. You should wait and be able to see me from here.'

Annabel said: 'I am coming with you; possibly there are more traps up there, you shouldn't go alone.' Mr H looked stern and said: 'No, I am going alone; you can see me all the time. I told you that something has protected us during our journey. You saw just a few minutes ago how we were protected: that incident was proof of my beliefs. I told you that we should believe in the horizon. I told you that it was going to be a unique experience. Tonight I am going to prove it to you again that our journey, and all these hardships that we've been through, were worth it and we are going to witness a miracle.' Annabel said again: 'I still believe some of us should be with you.'

'No, remember what the wise man said; I am the one that should go first, and that is final. You are better off sitting here and watching me. Just before I go, I need some dry wood. I want to make a fire up there so you can see me better.'

We all hunted around for dry wood and managed to find some. Before Mr H left he looked at us and said: 'Wish me luck. I am going to see the horizon; the end of the world. This is for all of us.' Then each one of us hugged him and wished him good luck. He was clearly shaking and so excited; he was only meters away from the end of our harsh and eventful journey. We all watched him with great fear and excitement. He made his way to the top of the mountain, to the horizon; the clear sky and moonlight helped us to see him clearly. When he arrived, he stopped and looked around, but it seemed there was nothing there. Several times he walked forward and back on the line of the horizon, but nothing happened. He shouted: 'Hey, I am here! My friends are also very close to you. We had a long and hard journey, only the hope of seeing you helped us to carry on. We are here, please show us a sign. You have already showed your spirit. I could feel you even before our journey. I was the one who insisted we had to get to you. Show us a sign! My friends and I have come from far away. Show us a sign! You just did it a short time ago: you rescued us from those evil people - please show us a sign.' But apart from the echo of his voice, there was no reply, nor any sign.

Mr H set two fires ten meters apart on the line of the horizon and started to walk between the fires, but nothing happened.

Annabel said sadly: 'He doesn't know what he wants; he is still in his paranoid world.'

Jolly responded: 'Wait, something may happen. Did you see how the armed men got killed? Did you see the light on the horizon? It must be something.'

Mr H paced between those fires on the line of the horizon for an hour, but there was no sign of Roxana or the spirit of spring. He started to shout again: 'Hey, we came here to see and feel the spirit of spring; we want to see Roxana, Goddess of Beauty. Roxana, you promised me that on the horizon you were going to dance with me. Tell us about our loved-ones. For years I have stuck to that damn river. Night after night I waited for a miracle that would help me to find my son. Roxana, Goddess of Beauty, you promised me on the nights of my consternation and in my journeys through Mark's nightmares that you would help me. You promised me that you would help my friends. Where are you now?' He was silent for some moments and than started to cry loudly and said: 'Roxana, Goddess of Beauty, please show us a sign. I have promised my friends that they are going to have a unique experience here. Where are you? I am tired; we are tired; tell us that there is another world where we can be happy and free from pain and sorrow. We are humans; tired of cells and torture, tired of bewilderment, show us the way to salvation!'

Sometime later he shook his head and said:

And human
Alas, have used to their pains of centuries   (22)

'Roxana, show us the way to heaven, rescue us from the pain of centuries!' But again nothing happened; he sank to his knees and continued to weep.

Annabel stopped looking at him and sat on a rock, holding her head in her hands. Now waves of disappointment and hopelessness washed over us. Helen came to me and said sadly: 'I am cold, can you start a fire here?' I made a fire and she sat next to it and stared at the flames silently. Minutes later she began to dance close to the fire. It was a strange dance; she was moving her hands and arms very close and over the fire. Jolly was staring sadly at the tree; she also started to move and dance close to the tree. Carol went to the edge of a rock and stared down at the valley, then she too, softly and strangely, started to dance. I remembered my stories: Carol was thinking of throwing herself from the heights; Helen was thinking of setting fire to herself; Jolly was thinking of hanging herself from the tree - and now they were dancing. It was the dance of death. Maybe Mr H also was thinking of throwing himself into a river. I was so scared. I shouted: 'You have promised that you are not going to do anything stupid.'

Mr H first looked at us and suddenly stood up and shouted: 'Okay Roxana, tonight I came here to have a dance with you, the dance of life, not the dance of death. Do you only make an appearance for the dance of death? Okay, come on, then, and have the last dance of death with me!' Then he took off his top clothes and shoes and scored his feet several times with his knife. Now blood was pouring out of his feet. He took up a wooden stick and began to dance; he was dancing like an Indian dancer and moving between the fires. It was an extraordinary scene. I remembered him when he was at the psychiatric hospital; he was acting like the Indian character in *One flew over the Cuckoo's Nest*. I looked at him and said to myself: 'This is splendidly strange and beautiful. How can he dance with his injured feet?' All of us stared at him and now every one of us was crying.

Moments later we heard the voice of a woman. She said: 'Enough of this dance of death, it is the time to dance to life!' and then she appeared on the line of the horizon. She was wearing a dress made of flowers and leaves. She was extremely beautiful. She came close to Mr H and took him in her arms and calmly said: 'I know you have come here from very far away, I know each one of you has had an extremely difficult journey, but you didn't go through all that for the sake of death. No - life brought you here; you should continue your lives. I know each one of you has had terrible experiences. In your journey you have witnessed all sorts of human suffering. By continuing with your lives you can help others.' And then she pointed at a big rock and said: 'Look!' Suddenly images of Arash, Shenya, Carol's husband and children, Annabel's husband and child and Mr H's son appeared on the rock. They were all surrounded by an aura of brightness. We stared at the images in complete shock. Within seconds, they all disappeared and Roxana said: 'You should accept the bitter reality that your loved ones are gone, but they are all at peace and have found tranquility. Carol, I know that you are a very talented actress; you should continue your profession: that is the best way to help yourself and others. Let others enjoy your talent and beauty. Annabel, you have had your revenge, it is the time for peace and calmness for you - and don't forget that there is a man who loves you very much. Helen, you are going to find your love, too, close to that river - and your children and Mr H need your help. Jolly, you have a daughter; this is the best reason for you to stay away from drugs. She needs your love and care. When you see her tell her that:

I would tell you to be patient
  to get involved without getting overwhelmed,
To give. To hold someone because it feels good
  to appreciate the subtleties which make you smile
To smile.

I would want you to fly
  with the particles of land and sky that soar,
To touch those peaks
  to endure those valleys.
Sorrow is inevitable... but so is happiness.

I would ask that you love
  Openly, honestly, freely, without attachment,
To enjoy that –
  you are a part of the cycle of life

The trees and wind and birds and sea.

I would hope that you experience
  playing, caring, sharing, discovering, fulfilling,
To go with that –
  Understanding, always trying
To live.

Then I would know that we had been comrades
  that would be good
To be sisters or sister and brother,
  lean on me when you're not strong
Our hands, embracing, clutching
Our eyes, forward, sparkling
Our minds, open, occupied
The whole world, our playground
(only, better than metal swings. We would have the real things.)
(23)

'My main message to all of you is: stop your obsession with the sky and take good care of your mother earth. She is the one that has given you everything. Mark, you are a great writer and your stories are going to be all over Hollywood. And finally I want to read you an inspirational poem. Jolly, you have heard it before: Arash has already read it to you. Now I want you all to listen to this carefully, this is a message from the spirit of spring:

Love creates love
Love donates life
Life begets toil
Toil creates anxious
Anxious donates trust
Trust, creates hope
Hope donates life
Life creates love
Love creates love (24)

'Now we must all dance to life,' and she started dancing with Mr H. They were dancing a waltz, I don't know if it was in our imagination or if it was real, but we could hear music too: it was a song called *Take This Waltz* sung by Leonard Cohen. It was a splendid scene again and I danced with each of the characters from my stories. Sometime later Roxana said: 'All of you should come to the horizon tomorrow after sunrise, and you will feel the spirit of spring.' Then she said goodbye, but before she left Mr H said to her in a loud voice so that we could also hear it:

Between eternal suns
Your beauty
Is an anchor
A sun that makes me free
From dawns of all stars   (25)

Minutes later Mr H came back to us. We were all very happy and excited. Each one of us thanked Mr H for his vision and leadership.

Immediately after sunrise we all went to the top of the mountain, to the horizon. Lots of beautiful wild flowers were scattered over the mountain. Mr H said: 'All of you, breathe deeply so you can feel the spirit of spring.' Then he continued: 'Last night I had the best time of my entire life - it was so amazing to dance with Roxana. When we were dancing she whispered the message of the spirit of spring into my ear and asked me to read it to you today. The message is:

We are wayfarers of dawns and mornings
Wayfarers of sunshine and twilight
Have no fear of our nights
Nor afflicted days and deep darkness
We are wayfarers of sunshine and twilight   (26)

For a couple of hours we enjoyed the horizon, and then Mr H said: 'Our journey shouldn't end here. Today each one of you is going to go your own way but we should keep in touch.'

Sometime later the wise man arrived on horseback. He smiled and said: 'I am glad that all of you made it. Now you can come to my place for more meditation. Now you are purified, you will enjoy the meditation even more.'

Mr H said: 'Dear wise man, you are better to take the ladies with you. Mark and I have to go back to the village to help Mohammad go back to his people. We will join you later.' Before they left, Carol came up to me and said: 'Could you send your stories to me? They are all good subjects for films.' I looked at her beautiful eyes and said: 'Yes of course. I am glad you have decided to carry on acting.' Moments later the wise man and the women mounted their horses and moved away from Mr H and me. When they reached another line on the horizon, at the top of another mountain in front of us, suddenly Mr H shouted: 'Hey ladies, this is for you, from us. From all men in the world, this is to show you that your love is life:

Your love that is life
Your fury that is death
***

You have reflected the hope of stars
In the hopelessness of skies
You have created years
Centuries
And gave birth to these men that have written on gallous
Memories
And the great history of hope of future
Is grown in your small womb
And you have created victory
In the uterus of the defeat
Your love that is life
Your fury that is death
***

You are shine of star's love
In the darkness and coldness of hearts
You are burner's glitter of kiss
In the thirsty ashes of lips
And you have thought us patient and strength under tortures
And in the miseries
Your love that is life
Your fury that is death
***

You are that are beautiful
And every man that goes anywhere
Worships the beauty
You are the sprit of life
And life without you is a cold kiln
The sprit's songs of your arms
Are amusing in the soul's ear of the men
Your love that is life
Your fury that is death
****

You have given men calmness in your arms
In the terrifying journey of life
And you have worshiped by any egotistical man
Give your love to us
Your love that is life
And give your fury to our enemies
Your fury that is death   (27)

108

His voice echoed beautifully in the mountains and I was sure that all the women were touched by his poem. For a moment they stopped and looked at us and then waved goodbye.

When the wise man and the women had gone, I stared into Mr H's eyes for a while. Surprised, he asked: 'Is there anything wrong?'

I blinked several times, and stared at him again. He said: 'Something wrong with your eyes again?'

'No, for seconds I saw an aureole around your head and face; you looked like a saint.'

'No, I am not a saint.'

I stared at him for little while and then started clapping him. He smiled and said: 'What is it? Why are you clapping?'

'You bastard son of a bitch, after your performance last night I really think you deserve the third one.'

'Third one of what?'

'Oscar, you bastard, you played a saint.'

'What are you talking about? Are you in your nightmares again? I thought after last night's events you had been cured.'

'Cured? Cured my ass, you just played God! Oh you bastard, you know how to charm the ladies ha? You may have fooled them but not me. This morning I saw some wires that were hidden behind some stones. I also saw cigarette butts all over the place; did you bring the film crews here? Early this morning I heard the sound of helicopters, did helicopters take them away? Did you fake it from the beginning?'

'No, I have read all your stories and I was with you in your nightmares, so I wanted to find a way to help you and the others. I had no idea what was going to happen on our journey, I just had an agreement with the wise man, and managed to contact my friends.'

'That was why he suggested that you became our leader and the first man to go to the horizon, ha?'

'Yes, and those three armed men were also faked; I had to create the belief that there was something extraordinary happening, so my friends helped me to do last night's scenes. Yes, you are right they came and left by helicopter. I didn't fool anybody. This is convincing.'

'But who gives you the right to play God?'

'I think that God is happier today; I have managed to help some very disturbed people.'

'By playing God?'

He angrily responded: 'Yes, look at you with all your characters! I suggest you stop writing and instead open a club and call it "suicide appreciation society" because most – if not all - of your characters have a tendency towards suicide. I have given them reason to carry on with their lives. I have used my expertise to promote life, not glorify death. I don't care if you accuse me of playing God; I used my acting ability to save lives. You know these women and their vulnerabilities better than anybody else. My friends in the film business and I helped them to appreciate life rather than glorify death - and yes I must admit our journey was the best experience of my career. My friends and I deserve much more than just an Oscar - we have saved lives. Now I can say I have truly lived; now death can come to me as well.'

'So you think I have glorified death do you? You are wrong. If in my writing I talk about misery and death, it is not because I am admiring death. This is all for the sake of humanity. Let me tell you part of a poem by a great poet: he said,
A mountain starts with the first stone
Being human begins with the first pain (28)
'Do you understand what he meant? It means that pain and death start from the very beginning of our lives. We should know them as well as anything else; actually, knowing them helps us to appreciate life more.'

Mr H put his hand companionably on my shoulder and said: 'I am glad that is over now; I was worried that they might harm themselves.'

We walked towards the village to collect Mohammad. On our way I smiled and said: 'So, I am a great writer and my stories are going to be all over Hollywood, ha?'

He smiled and said: 'I'll do my best to take you to an Oscar ceremony - sorry about last time. Was it very heavy to carry those boxes?'

'Yes it was, very heavy, I think my balls are as big as yours now. Don't worry about the Oscar ceremony; I have been there already and won lots of awards.'

'How?'

'I told you before that I have got a vivid imagination, so with my imagination I can go everywhere and be close to anything - although it can't be exactly the same as the real thing, but very close to it. Every time I write a novel, I imagine it's going to be published and that Hollywood is going to make a film out of it, and the actors or directors of my stories are going to win awards. Their win would be my win too. I don't think that there is any place for a novelist in the Oscar ceremony. I know there is something for screen-writers but not for novelists. Anyway all the glory and money is going to people like you and the directors, and people like me with the difficult and lonely job of writing are ignored. Don't get me wrong, I know acting is very difficult. Sometimes getting into the shoes of someone else's creation and trying to give them life is more difficult than creating the original idea, but I still believe that writers' work should be appreciated more.'

'What about acting? Do you want to act? You have a good eye for detecting good acting.'

'I am acting all the time - we all do - but acting as a profession...no, I'd better stick to my writing. And I wasn't joking that you deserve that third Oscar for participating in our journey and for last night's act - you were brilliant.'

He looked at me seriously and said: 'It wasn't just acting, it was something else. I could feel some very strong force during our journey. It wasn't just acting: when I got to the Horizon for the first time, I could see something extraordinary.

'Yes, you saw your beautiful fellow actress, who was she?'

'Her name is Michel, she is a talented actress.'

'Yes, I noticed. Michel is also the name of one of the characters in my unfinished story; sometimes I have named her Roxana. So you have read all my stories, ha?'

'Yes, I have read them all, including the unfinished one *Poem and War*, but I told you it wasn't just acting when I got to the horizon, I felt and saw an extraordinary thing.'

'What? What did you see?'

'I saw...'

Part (6)
Back to Nightmarish Realities
Wiser

'Wake up, wake up; it is time for you to get some discipline' – when I was in military high school.

'Wake up, wake up; the attack has started' – when I was in the war between Iran and Iraq.

'Wake up, wake up; they are coming to arrest you' – when I was an escapee and hiding in Iran.

'Wake up, wake up; it's your turn to be tortured' – when I was in a prison in Iraq.

'Wake up, wake up; they are going to fuck you' – when I was in another prison in Iraq.

'Wake up, wake up; they are going to deport you to hell again' – when I was in a detention centre at the airport in London.

'Wake up, wake up; I know you are awake, welcome to the real nightmare.'

'Oh you fucking Voice!' I opened my eyes. I was lying down on the top of a mountain; on the horizon, the first thing I saw was blue sky and a vast emptiness. I looked at it for some time. I remembered Mr H's last unfinished sentence. I think I know the words to complete his sentence: vast emptiness, yes: *vast emptiness* is what would complete his sentence. Roxana was right; we should stop our obsession with the sky and love and take care of our mother earth.

Moments later, I felt some drops of water on my head. I turned my head and I saw a beautiful wild flower close to my head; the water-drops I felt were the dew of that flower. I looked at its beauty, maybe the flower was growing at the heart of the earth and was nourished by the blood of the earth. Was the earth crying blood? Lorca was right when he wrote:

Flowers are dying from the love
Flowers are dying from the love   **(29)**

The End

References

I would like to mention that apart from my own poems, the rest of them are free translation of other poets.

(1)-By Lorca
(2)-By Lorca
(3)-By Lorca
(4)- By Mark Hill
(5)- By Shamlu (Iranian poet)
(6)- By Mark Hill
(7)- By Shamlu
(8)- By Mark Hill
(9)- By Mark Hill
(10)- By Mark Hill
(11)- Part of an Iranian's song by Nosrat Farzanh
(12)- By Shamlu
(13)- By Shamlu (slightly changed)
(14)- By Shamlu
(15)- By Mark Hill
(16)- By Langston Hughes
(17)- By Shamlu (slightly changed)
(18)- By Shamlu
(19)- By Federico Garcia Lorca, translated by Martin Sorrell
(20)- By Shamlu
(21)- By an Iranian poet
(22)- By Shamlu
(23)-By Morgan
(24)- By Margot Bickel
(25)- By Shamlu
(26)- By Langston Hughes
(27)- By Shamlu
(28)- By Shamlu
(29)- By Federico Garcia Lorca